HISTORY OF THE META-KRANCH WAR

Eons ago, on a planet called Nacrum in the galaxy of Rathmor, what came to be known as the Great Hunt began. The Metas, a barbaric race of shape-shifting aliens, whose only joy was destruction and dominion, declared terminal open season on the Kranch, another alien species. The Kranch had developed a peace-loving society that was unwilling to shed the blood of their enemies. To protect both themselves and their young from the fearsome Metas, these peaceful aliens were forced into hiding.

Over the centuries, with a depleted number of Kranch to hunt and a growing blood thirst, the Metas began conquering the inhabitants of surrounding planets and galaxies. Nearly invincible, there was very little any creature could do to stop them. Realizing the staggering amount of lost lives and holding the only effective weapon against the Metas, the Kranch appointed a few of themselves as Protectors. These Protector Kranch steered aggression away from the inhabited colonies of the universe and focused it on themselves instead. While dangerous for the Protectors, they knew it was for the greater good.

So it came to pass that on one of these protectorate missions a Kranch vessel was disabled as it entered the Milky Way galaxy. And so our story begins...

Decoy™

No. 1

$2.75 US
$4.25 CAN
MAR.'99

Mini-Series
1 of 4

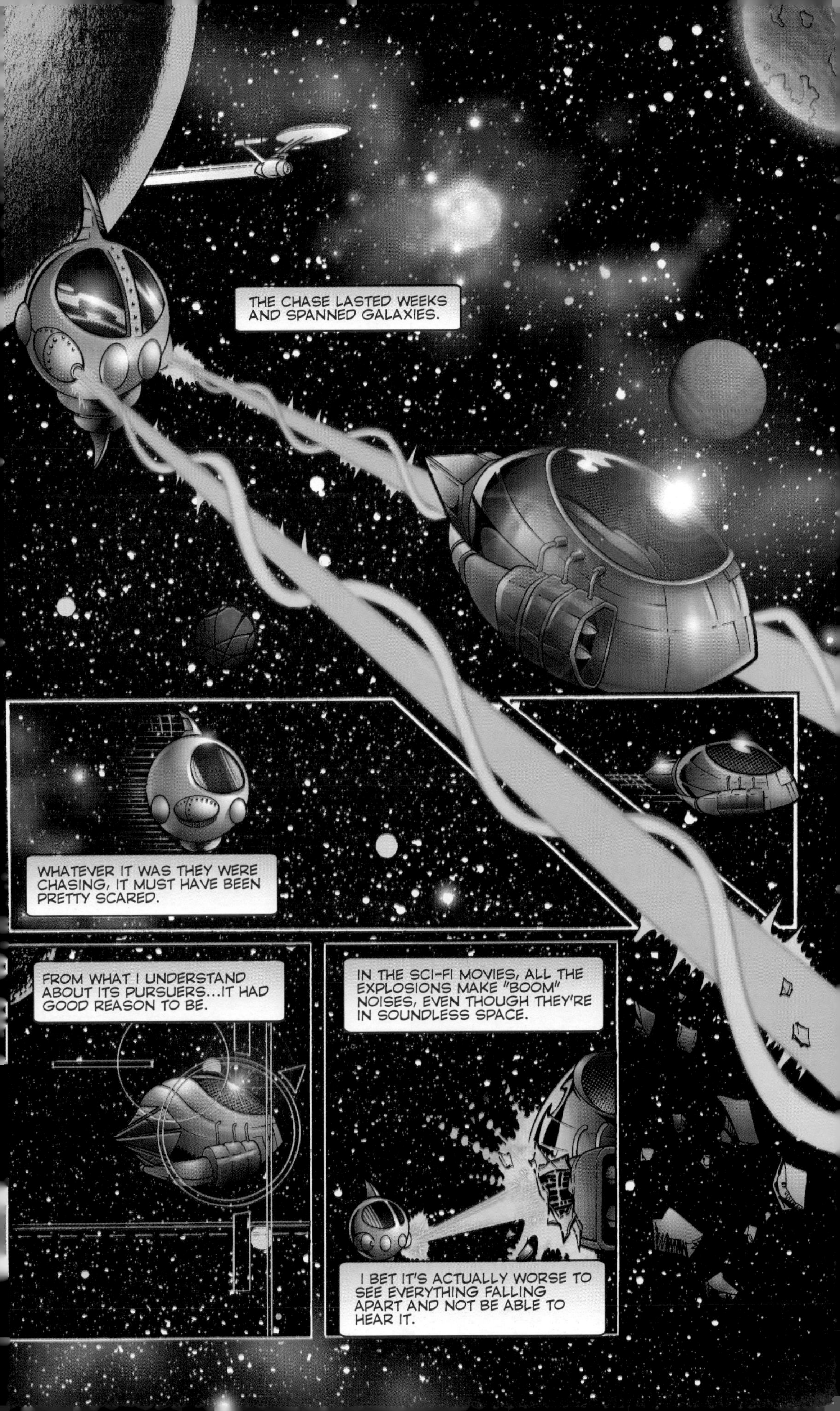
THE CHASE LASTED WEEKS AND SPANNED GALAXIES.
WHATEVER IT WAS THEY WERE CHASING, IT MUST HAVE BEEN PRETTY SCARED.
FROM WHAT I UNDERSTAND ABOUT ITS PURSUERS...IT HAD GOOD REASON TO BE.
IN THE SCI-FI MOVIES, ALL THE EXPLOSIONS MAKE "BOOM" NOISES, EVEN THOUGH THEY'RE IN SOUNDLESS SPACE.
I BET IT'S ACTUALLY WORSE TO SEE EVERYTHING FALLING APART AND NOT BE ABLE TO HEAR IT.

I'M NOT REAL CLEAR ON THE TIMES HERE, BUT I WOULD GUESS RIGHT ABOUT NOW, I WAS GETTING TO WORK.

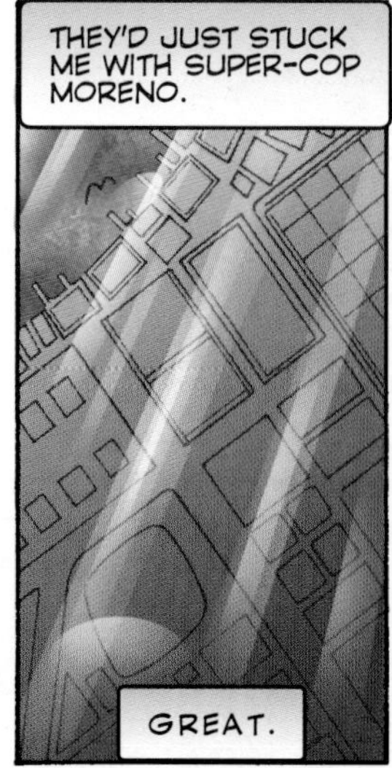
THEY'D JUST STUCK ME WITH SUPER-COP MORENO.
GREAT.

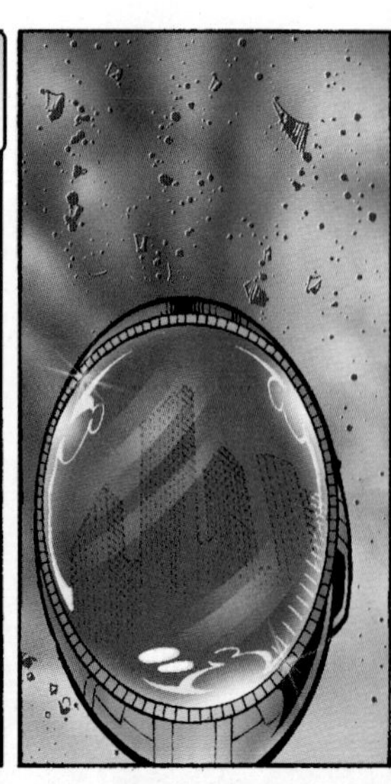

AND THEN, LATER THAT DAY, I'D BE BUSY GETTING MYSELF KILLED.

SALE!
BUT EVEN BEFORE THEN, I'D HEARD ABOUT THE SIGHTING. EVERYONE WAS TALKING ABOUT IT THAT DAY.

KINDA EARLY FOR *FIREWORKS*, *AIN'T* IT, ROY?
I RECKON.

NO WAY, DUDE! THAT THING'S REAL! I TOLD YOU THEY'RE OUT THERE! I TOLD YOU ART BELL WAS RIGHT!
LOOK! UP IN THE SKY! IT'S A B--
DON'T EVEN GO THERE.
WOW! IS SOMEONE SHOOTING A MOVIE AROUND HERE?
YOU LISTEN TO WAY TOO MUCH TALK RADIO.

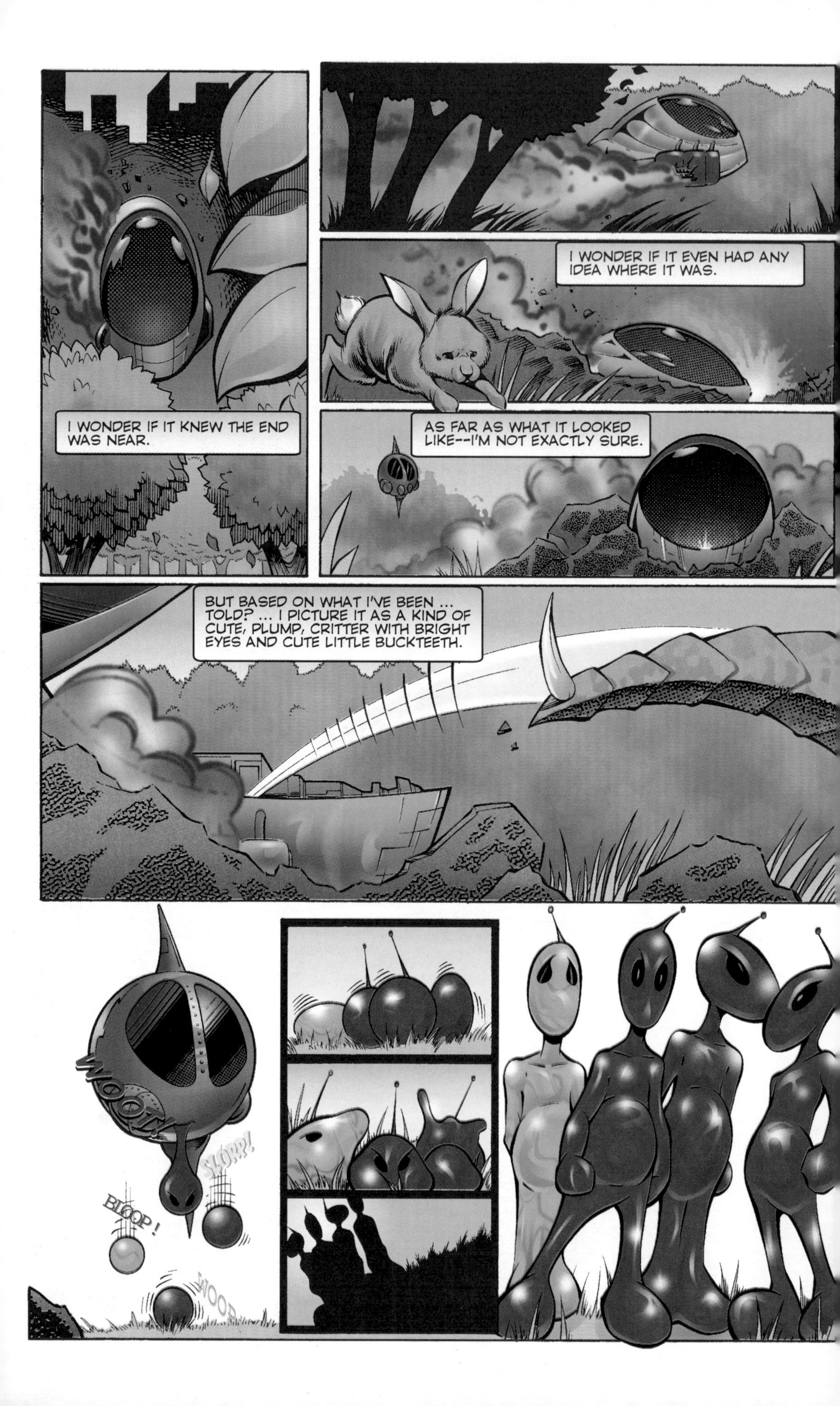
I WONDER IF IT KNEW THE END WAS NEAR.
I WONDER IF IT EVEN HAD ANY IDEA WHERE IT WAS.
AS FAR AS WHAT IT LOOKED LIKE--I'M NOT EXACTLY SURE.
BUT BASED ON WHAT I'VE BEEN ... TOLD? ... I PICTURE IT AS A KIND OF CUTE, PLUMP, CRITTER WITH BRIGHT EYES AND CUTE LITTLE BUCKTEETH.
WOOT!
SLORP!
BLOOP!
WOOP

ANYWAY, THE POOR THING WAS THEIR PREY.
AND THEY WERE TOO POWERFUL AND TOO AGGRESSIVE TO BE FOUGHT BY CREATURES OF HIS PEACEFUL NATURE.
WHAK!

YOU WOULDN'T GUESS THAT THOSE LITTLE THINGS COULD BE SUCH FIERCE COMBATANTS, BUT THERE'S STRENGTH IN NUMBERS, I GUESS.
ESPECIALLY WHEN IT'S THREE TO ONE.

ALTHOUGH I THINK THEY WERE COUNTING ON FOUR TO ONE.

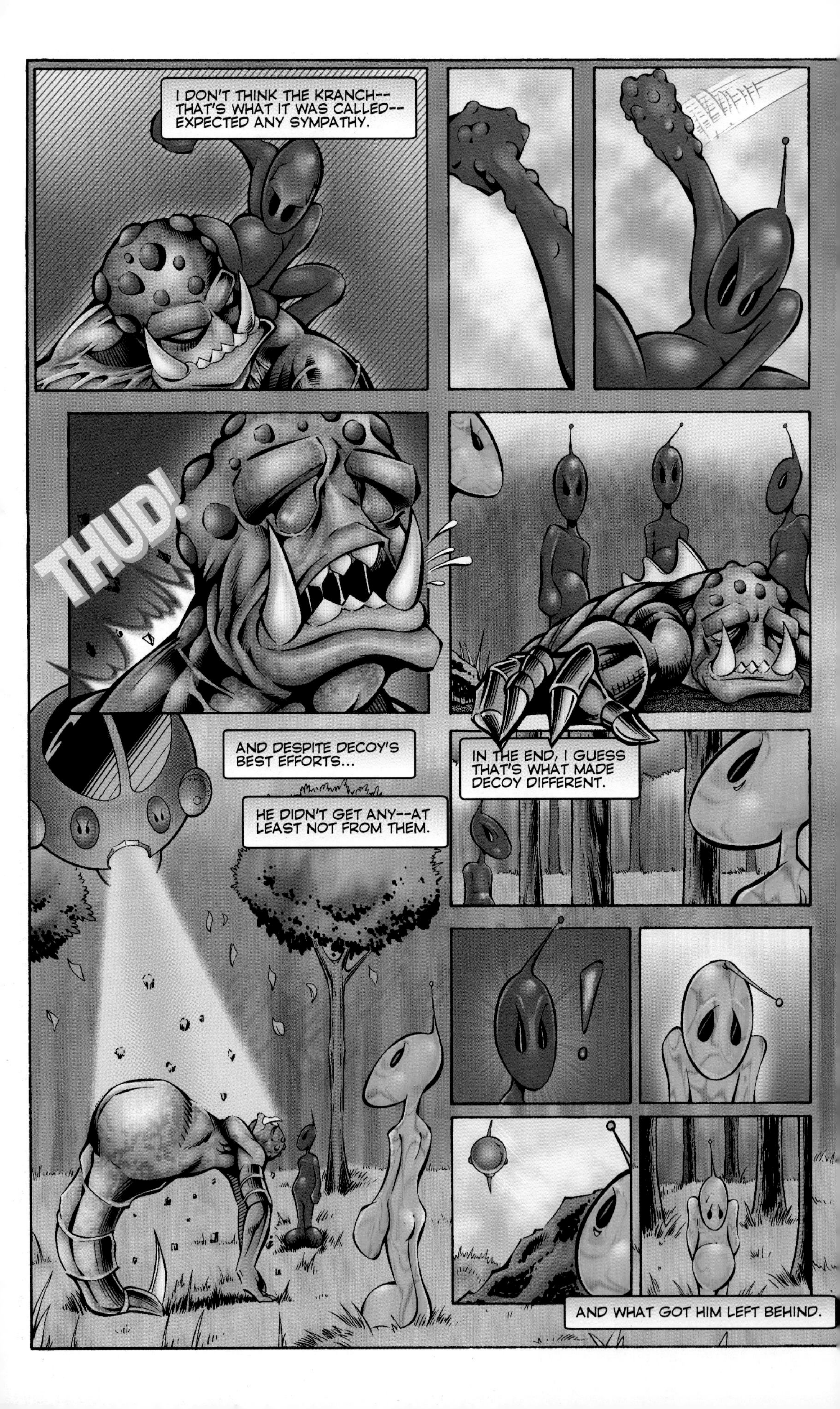
I DON'T THINK THE KRANCH--
THAT'S WHAT IT WAS CALLED--
EXPECTED ANY SYMPATHY.
THUD!
AND DESPITE DECOY'S
BEST EFFORTS...
HE DIDN'T GET ANY--AT
LEAST NOT FROM THEM.
IN THE END, I GUESS
THAT'S WHAT MADE
DECOY DIFFERENT.
!
AND WHAT GOT HIM LEFT BEHIND.

SOMEWHERE ELSE ENTIRELY, I WAS ABOUT TO BE INVOLVED IN A CHASE OF MY OWN.
BUB LITE
RESTROOM
THAT'S IT. WE TRIED TO BE NICE.
LOOK I DON'T CARE IF YOU GUYS DID JUST GET OUT OF PRISON YESTERDAY, I'M NOT GIVING YOU A FREE DRINK!
WHY DON'T YOU TWO FIND SOME SLEAZY DIVE THAT CATERS TO THE CRIMINAL ELEMENT? JUST GET OUT OF HERE!
ALL YOUR CASH-IN A BAG.
NOW.
UH ...!
SLAM!
CALL THE POLICE!
SLAM!
WHOOPS!
WHAT DO YOU MEAN, "WHOOPS?"
COPS!
WHERE'S YOUR GUN?
DROPPED IT!
YOU IDIOT! IT'S HER! THE ONE I TOLD YOU ABOUT!

I CAN'T *BELIEVE* SHE'S GONNA GET ME *AGAIN!*
SHE'S JUST A *CHICK!* HOW *HUFF-KAFF* TOUGH CAN SHE *BE?*
FINE. *YOU* TAKE HER ON THIS TIME.
A BUGS WAR
COMING SOON...
GIVE IT *UP*, LOSERS! I'M ON YA!
WORKING *ALONE*, ARE YOU? I'M NOT *EVEN* HERE, RIGHT?

C'MON, FRANK, YOU'RE MAKING THIS HARDER THAN LAST TIME!

WE GOTTA SPLIT UP! WE'LL MEET BACK LATER!

THEY'RE SPLITTING! YOU TAKE THAT ONE!

WHO ARE YOU ORDERING AROUND, LUCK? YOU -- OH, FORGET IT.

IT'S COOL ... SHE'S JUST A CHICK. I'M NOT GONNA GET ...

... CAUGHT.
OOOOFF!!
FWUMPA!

JERK.

YOU WANT SOME? FINE! I JUST GOT OUT OF THE HOLE ...

SHMAK!
... AND NO PUNK LIKE YOU IS SENDIN' ME BACK!

THAM!
YOU CAN'T--
OOO-OOOF!
AURGH!
K-MAK!
SHTAK!
MMMPH!
YES, I CAN. AND LOOK AT THAT-- YOU ALMOST MADE ME BREAK A NAIL.
YOU'RE LUCKY--
THIS TIME.
YOU HAVE THE RIGHT TO REMAIN SILENT.

HA! THIS IS TOO EASY! YOU SURE YOU'RE A REAL COP?
SMAT-K!
AARGH!

TMAK!
AT LEAST YOUR PARTNER KNOWS HOW TO THROW A PUNCH!

AND TAKE ONE!
TH-KOW!

ANYTHING YOU'D LIKE TO ADD? NO? GOOD.
LOSER.
NOW, WHERE DID I DROP THAT BAG OF ...

YEAH, I'VE GOT SOMETHING TO ADD.
THAM!
I KNOW HOW TO THROW A PUNCH, TOO!

NO, REALLY, YOU LOOK LOVELY.
STOP IT.
I'M JUST SAYING BLACK AND BLUE IS A GOOD COLOR SCHEME FOR YOU. YOU SHOULD GET BEATEN UP MORE OFTEN.
KNOCK IT OFF, OK?
SQUAWK!
YEAH, WE'VE BEEN HAVING PROBLEMS WITH THEM FOR MONTHS.
UNIT FOUR ADAM TWELVE TO DISPATCH -- ARGH! WORTHLESS RADIOS!
D-COY 1
I'M SO GLAD THIS IS MY LAST DAY OF PARTNERING WITH YOU. I CAN'T WAIT TO SEE WHO MY REAL PARTNER WILL BE.
CHEE, THAT'S TOO BAD, MORENO. YOU TWO MAKE SUCH A CUTE COUPLE.
WEREN'T YOU TOLD ABOUT YOUR RIGHT TO REMAIN SILENT?

LUCK! MORENO! BOOK YOUR GUYS AND GET OVER HERE!
BUT SHE SWEARS SHE SAW IT!
I'M TELLIN' YA -- IT WAS A WEATHER BALLOON OR SOMETHING.
YEAH, I'VE HEARD THAT BEFORE!

THE CAPTAIN WANTS YOU TWO.

TOGETHER!

YOU TWO! HOLD IT!
THERE'S BEEN A ROSTER CHANGE.
I HATE THAT GUY.
MISSING

CARTER'S BACK IN THE HOSPITAL AND EVANS LEFT THE FORCE, SO --
EVANS QUIT?!

WHAT THIS MEANS IS YOU TWO WILL BE PARTNERED UP.
KILL ME, GOD. KILL ME NOW.
PERMANENTLY.

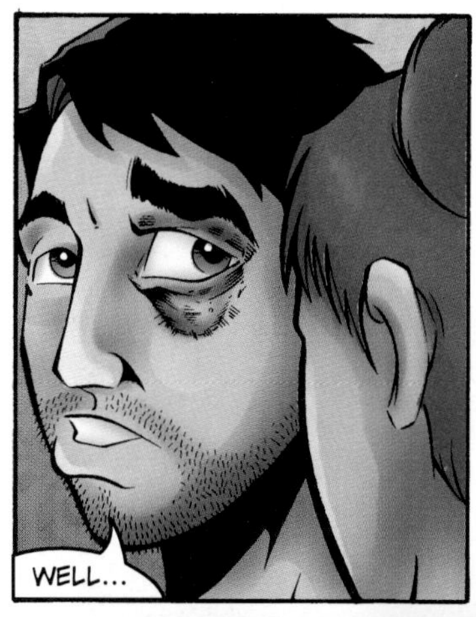
WELL...

I GUESS *THAT'S* OK WITH ME, IF --

IT DOESN'T *HAVE* TO BE *OK* WITH YOU!
THIS ISN'T A CHOICE, *IT'S AN ORDER!*

ULP! YES, SIR. I'M ... UH ... GONNA CHECK MY MESSAGES.

WITH ALL DUE *RESPECT*, SIR, YOU CAN'T BE SERIOUS!
THERE'S NO *WAY* I CAN WORK WITH THAT ARROGANT, IMMATURE, SELF-CENTERED ...

LET'S SEE...
CLARENCE.
CLARENCE.
CLARENCE.

WHAT'S *THIS*?

T. MORENO --
Call Billy Two-Ranks.
HOT TIP!!
on Nabob Gang
555-0162

THIS IS *BIG*. I COULD--

HELLO? BILLY?
NO, *SORRY*, SHE'S NOT AVAILABLE, BUT SHE WANTED ME TO *CALL* YOU. WHATTAYA GOT?

WHY GIVE ME A PATROLMAN PARTNER? I'M ON THE SHORT LIST TO MAKE DETECTIVE!

THAT'S NOT THE ONLY LIST YOU'RE GOING TO BE ON IF YOU KEEP GIVING ME GRIEF!
BESIDES, YOU TWO HAVE ACTUALLY DONE SOME DECENT WORK TOGETHER.

BUT HE'S IMPOSSIBLE! HE DOESN'T KNOW THE MEANING OF TEAMWORK!

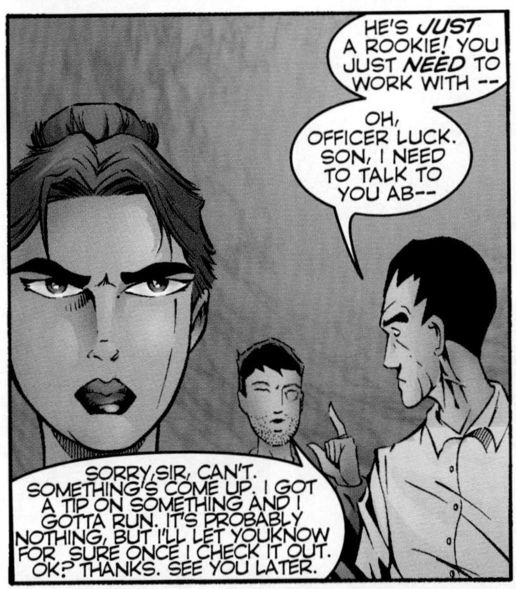
HE'S JUST A ROOKIE! YOU JUST NEED TO WORK WITH --
OH, OFFICER LUCK. SON, I NEED TO TALK TO YOU AB--
SORRY,SIR, CAN'T. SOMETHING'S COME UP. I GOT A TIP ON SOMETHING AND I GOTTA RUN. IT'S PROBABLY NOTHING, BUT I'LL LET YOUKNOW FOR SURE ONCE I CHECK IT OUT. OK? THANKS. SEE YOU LATER.

DON'T SAY IT.

UFOS! I KNEW IT!
MAYBE THEY'VE COME TO TAKE MARILYN MANSON BACK HOME WITH THEM.
THIS IS MY BIG CHANCE! I'LL SHOW 'EM!

NO MORE "OUT OF LUCK" JOKES! NO MORE HEARING ABOUT ROOKIE MISTAKES! WHEN I BUST THE NABOB GANG, THEY'LL SEE WHAT I'M MADE OF!

HOW *HARD* CAN THIS BE? ALREADY CAUGHT TWO *BAD* GUYS-- BLACK EYE TO PROVE IT.
NO *BIG* DEAL--STAY *CALM*. JUST BREATHE.
I *AM* THE MAN!
ROOKIE OF THE YEAR.
YEAH, *RIGHT*.
D-COY1

I ALMOST *FEEL* SORRY FOR THESE CLOWNS.

I BET I'LL GET A PROMOTION!

I *AM* THE MAN!

OK ... THIS LOOKS RIGHT.
I'LL STOP HERE.
NO NEED TO DRIVE RIGHT UP AND ANNOUNCE MYSELF.

LOOKS *QUIET* ENOUGH.

I *CAN'T* BELIEVE I STOLE TESSA'S TIP! IF SHE FINDS OUT...
I'M THROUGH.

HMMMM ... LET'S TRY THIS WAY.

OK, NO TIME TO GET NERVOUS. THEY'RE ALL MINE.
I *AM* THE MAN.
I *AM* THE MAN.
I *AM* THE MAN.
SKRITCHIT
WHO'S THERE?
STUPID SQUIRREL!
COOL. NO ONE'S COMING.
HERE WE GO. TIRE TRACKS. IT SHOULDN'T BE MUCH FARTHER TO THE --
-- PLACE.

WOW, THERE ARE A LOT OF PEOPLE IN THERE.
MAYBE GETTING BACK-UP WOULD BE A GOOD IDEA.
WELL, AT LEAST NO ONE'S SEEN ME YET.

DOES THAT IDIOT ACTUALLY THINK NO ONE CAN SEE HIM?
APPARENTLY SO, SIR.
WHERE'S TESSA MORENO? WE THOUGHT MORENO WAS COMING, NOT THIS ... THIS ...

HE'LL APPARENTLY HAVE TO DO. METHANE, WE WANT YOU TO TAKE CARE OF HIM. STATION YOURSELF OUTSIDE, THOUGH, SO WE DON'T SOUR THE DEAL.

MY PLEASURE, SIR.

KRUST-CKLE!
KRTCH-ACK!
THIS IS OFFICER LUCK TO DISPATCH, REQUEST BACK-UP AT --
HAND-HELD RADIOS ARE SCREWING UP, TOO! WHEN ARE THEY GOING TO GET THESE THINGS REPLACED?
WELL, I WANTED THIS ONE ALL TO MYSELF.
LET'S SEE WHAT WE HAVE HERE.
WELL, WHADDYA KNOW?

I DON'T KNOW WHAT'S GOING ON HERE, BUT THAT GUY WITH THE HAIR LOOKS A LOT LIKE DR. ALLOY. SOMETHING BAD IS GOING DOWN!
YES, YES! I TOLD YOU I'D DO IT! EVERYTHING'S READY FOR THE CONFERENCE! NOW, PLEASE GIVE ME THE MONEY!
JUST SO LONG AS WE'RE CLEAR ...
IF ANYTHING HAPPENS TO THE PLAN ...
SOMETHING HAPPENS TO YOU. GET IT?
I ... YES.
GOOD.
ALL RIGHT! NOBODY MOVE! YOU'RE ALL UNDER ARREST!
NO, PLEASE, NO.
I'VE ALREADY CALLED FOR BACK-UP SO DON'T EVEN THIN OF DOING ANYTHING!
NOW, UP AGAINS THE WALL! ALL OF YA

MY FIRST BUST AND I'D GOTTEN THE INFAMOUS DR. ALLOY.
OK, KEEP COOL, YOU'RE DOING IT.
THE WALL! NOW! MOVE! YOU'RE ALL COMING WITH ME!
OH, REEEEAAALLLY?

I BEG TO DIFFER.

PAL, IF YOU THINK THESE LITTLE THINGS ARE GOING TO STOP ME, YOU'VE GOT A LOT OF --

RUN!
WHAT? WHAT'S --
FORGET THIS! I'M OUTTA HERE!

KA-WHUMPA-TOOOMMMM!!
TSKCH!
KRKA-BOOM!
YOU WITH THE CASE! GET BACK HERE!

I LOST SIGHT OF THE OTHER TWO, BUT NOT WATERSON.
OHGOD-PLEASEGET-MEOUTTATHIS
AAAAAHHHHH!
GLORP!
PLEASE, I SWEAR I'LL NEVER DO ANYTHING ILLEGAL AGAIN.
TRISTL-TRISTL!
I WON'T DRIVE FAST... I'LL NEVER THROW MY TRASH ON THE HIGHWAY AGAIN!
JUST GET ME OUT OF THIS!
THRUNCH!
HE ACTUALLY THOUGHT HE WAS GETTING AWAY.
HUNH-HUNH-HUNH
THRUNCH!

HUNH-HUNH-HUNH-HA-HA!
IN FACT, ALL HE DID WAS MAKE A CIRCLE AROUND BACK TO WHERE HE STARTED, AND THAT WAS ALL THE BREAK I NEEDED.

BAMMM

PLEASE, YOU DON'T UNDERSTAND...

HE WAS RIGHT. ALL I UNDERSTOOD WAS THAT I WAS RIDING HIGH.
YOU'RE UNDER ARREST FOR ASSOCIATING WITH KNOWN FUGITIVES AND EVADING ARREST.
YOU WANT TO HELP YOURSELF? YOU GIVE ME SOME INFORMATION ABOUT WHAT'S GOING ON HERE, AND MAYBE I CAN GO EASY ON YOU.
I'VE GOT A BETTER IDEA.

I'LL GIVE YOU SOME BULLETS AND YOU LET HIM GO.
DEAL? GOOD.

UH-OH ...

K-BLAMM!

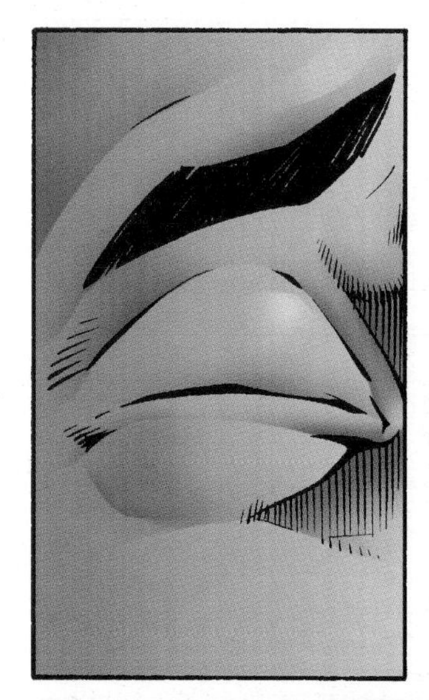

I REMEMBER HEARING THE FAINT SOUNDS OF HIS APPROACH.

I DON'T REALLY RECALL MY LAST THOUGHTS, BUT I'M SURE THEY WERE FILLED WITH THE ODD MIX OF SADNESS AND WONDER AT ACTUALLY SEEING A CREATURE FROM ANOTHER PLANET.
GREAT. THE ANGEL OF DEATH IS MADE OUT OF GREEN SILLY PUTTY.

HE LOOKED BACK AT ME ...

... AND THEN I DIED.
TO BE CONTINUE

Art by Allen Gooding and Rober Quijiano

No. 2

$2.75 US
$4.25 CAN
APR. '99

MINI-SERIES
2 of 4

POLICE

Huddleston &
ALMOND 12-98

DREAMS ARE ALWAYS STRANGE...
MASON ST.
NOOOOOO!
THIS USED TO BE SUCH A QUIET NEIGHBOR-HOOD.

OF COURSE, THEN THERE'S REALITY...
PFP...
3:16
AUSTI
WORLD WRESTLIN'
THE TRUTH IS OUT THERE...
D
NO, WAIT --
... AND OFFICIALS HAVE OFFERED NO EXPLANATIONS FOR THE OBJECTS SPOTTED YESTERDAY IN THE SKIES ABOVE DOLPHIN CITY, ALTHOUGH SOURCES SAY THERE IS NO TRUTH TO RUMORS ALIENS HAVE LANDED IN OR NEAR OUR FAIR CITY. ANNE?
VICTORIAN MYTHICS
LITTLE GREEN MEN, RUNNING AROUND DOLPHIN CITY? I DON'T THINK SO. THANKS, RICHARD.
THAT CAN SOMETIMES MAKE THOSE STRANGEST OF DREAMS SEEM ALMOST NORMAL.

...I'M HOME?
I'M ALIVE? DID I DREAM GETTING SHOT IN THE WOODS?
NO, I KNOW IT HAPPENED!
THERE WAS DR. ALLOY, AND THE GUY WITH THE BRIEFCASE--BUT SOMEHOW...
I'M ALIVE!
YEAH, BABY, YEAH!
HEH, HEH!
OH, MAN, I WAS SUPPOSED TO BE ON-DUTY AN HOUR AGO.
I'M DEAD.

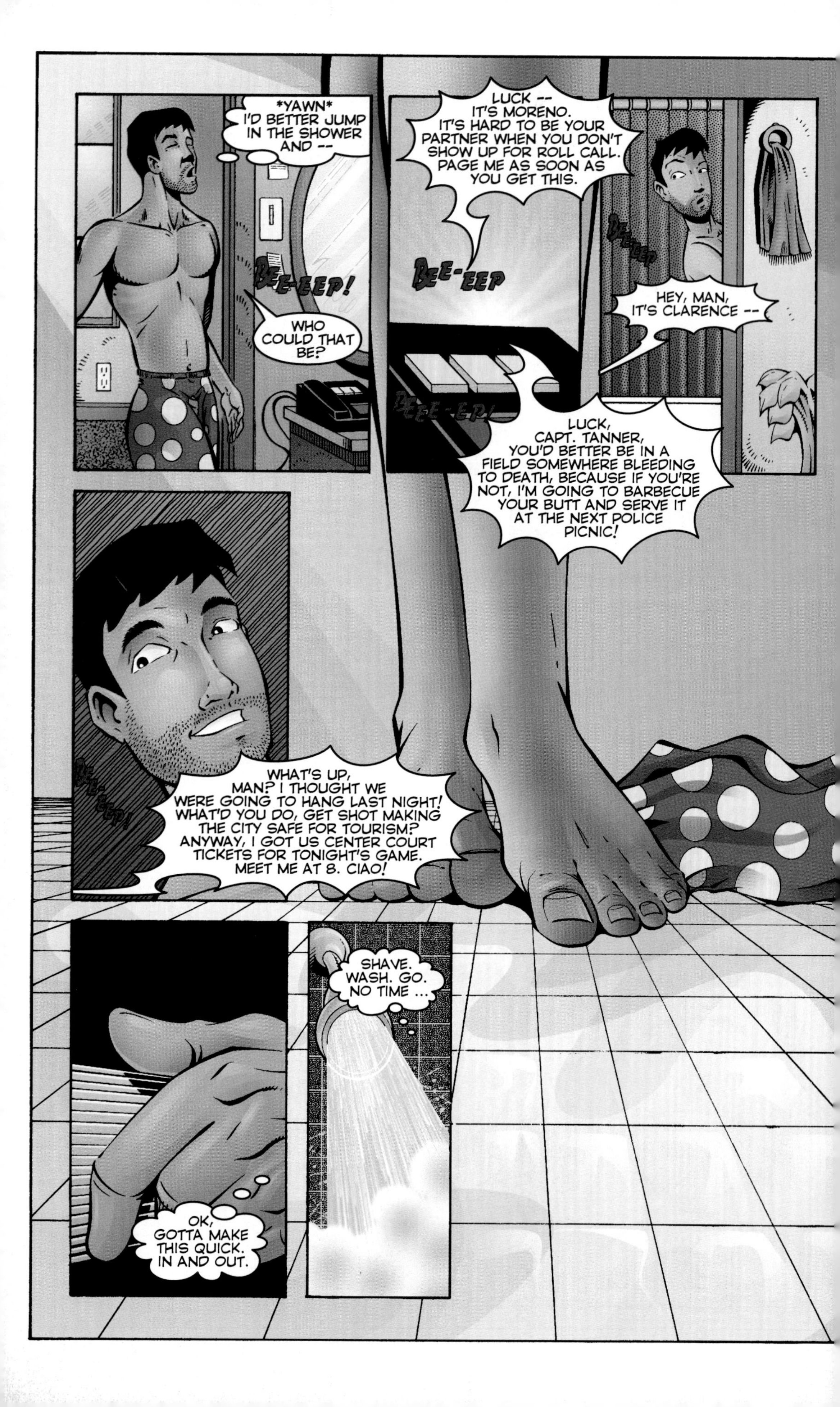
YAWN
I'D BETTER JUMP IN THE SHOWER AND --
BEE-EEEP!
WHO COULD THAT BE?
LUCK -- IT'S MORENO. IT'S HARD TO BE YOUR PARTNER WHEN YOU DON'T SHOW UP FOR ROLL CALL. PAGE ME AS SOON AS YOU GET THIS.
BEE-EEP
HEY, MAN, IT'S CLARENCE --
LUCK, CAPT. TANNER, YOU'D BETTER BE IN A FIELD SOMEWHERE BLEEDING TO DEATH, BECAUSE IF YOU'RE NOT, I'M GOING TO BARBECUE YOUR BUTT AND SERVE IT AT THE NEXT POLICE PICNIC!
WHAT'S UP, MAN? I THOUGHT WE WERE GOING TO HANG LAST NIGHT! WHAT'D YOU DO, GET SHOT MAKING THE CITY SAFE FOR TOURISM? ANYWAY, I GOT US CENTER COURT TICKETS FOR TONIGHT'S GAME. MEET ME AT 8. CIAO!
OK, GOTTA MAKE THIS QUICK. IN AND OUT.
SHAVE. WASH. GO. NO TIME ...

OK, HOW AM I GOING TO EXPLAIN THIS?
ABDUCTED BY ALIENS? THEY'LL THINK I'M CRAZY.
THE TRUTH? I WAS CHASING A SUSPECT WHEN A GUY IN A GASMASK SHOT ME, BUT I MIRACULOUSLY MADE IT BACK HOME, ALTHOUGH I DON'T KNOW HOW?
WHAT TH --
DANG, I'M LOSIN' IT.
MAYBE I DO NEED TO BE LOCKED AWAY.
WELL, RIGHT NOW ALL I NEED TO WORRY ABOUT IS HOW I'M GOING TO KEEP CAPT. TANNER FROM TEARING MY HEAD OFF.

HEH, HEH, HEH, LITTLE GREEN MEN.
YEAH, RIGHT!

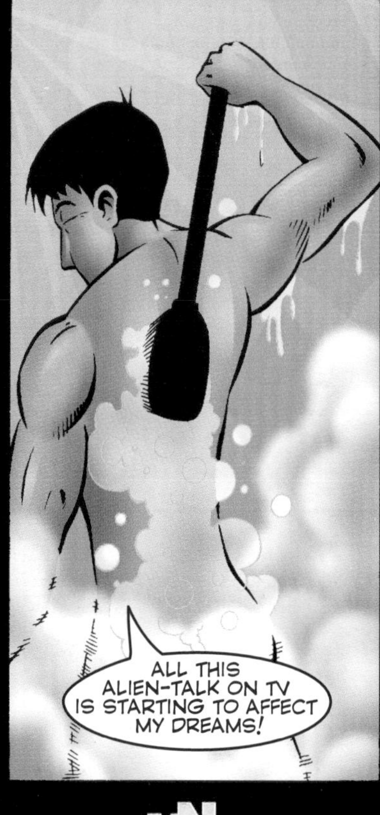
ALL THIS ALIEN-TALK ON TV IS STARTING TO AFFECT MY DREAMS!

ROCK ON ROSWELL! THE ALIENS HAVE LANDED!

KNOCK
KNOCK

NOW WHAT?

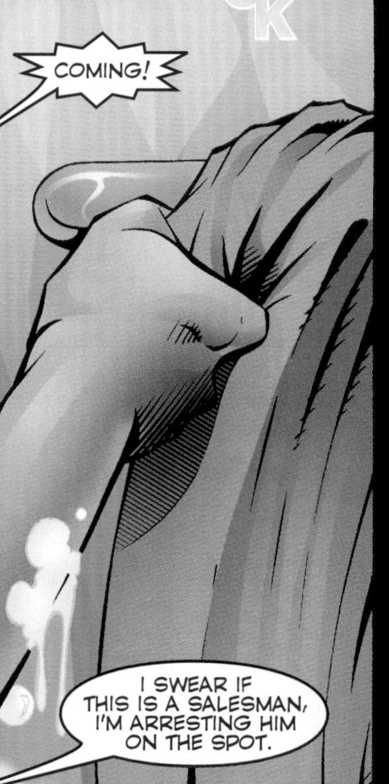
COMING!
I SWEAR IF THIS IS A SALESMAN, I'M ARRESTING HIM ON THE SPOT.

KNOCK
I SAID I'M COMING!
GEEZ.

OFFICER
-UCK! HOW NICE TO SEE YOU! REMEMBER ME?
YOUR PARTNER?
Unfortunately.

WHAT ARE YOU DOING HERE, MORENO?

GET DRESSED, TANNER WANTS YOU.
ALL RIGHT, JUST A SECOND.

BY THE WAY, WHAT HAPPENED TO YOUR BLACK EYE? IT'S ALREADY GONE.
HUH?

PROBABLY WEARING MORE MAKEUP THAN ME.

SO HOW MAD IS TANNER? WHAT'D HE SAY?
I HEARD "CROSSING GUARD."

READY TO DIRECT TRAFFIC? YOU KNOW HOW BAD RUSH HOUR CAN GET!
SHUT UP!

SO LET ME GET THIS STRAIGHT-YOU HAVE NO IDEA HOW YOUR PATROL CAR GOT BACK TO THE STATION?
NOPE. ALL I REMEMBER IS BEING IN THIS FIELD, CHASING A GUY, AND THEN I ... I ...
YOU'D BETTER COME UP WITH A BETTER STORY THAN THAT FOR CAPTAIN TANNER.
I JUST CAN'T FIGURE OUT -- HUH?
WHAT WAS THAT?
UH ... UH ... NOTHING?

7-ADAM-11 ON A *SQKRRTCHT* --ED ROBBERY AT 21ST AND BALL. SUSPECT IS *SKREEEEEEEEEE----*
THEY HAVE GOT TO DO SOMETHING ABOUT THESE RADIOS!
21ST AND BALL ... THAT'S JUST A COUPLE OF BLOCKS OVER FROM HERE.
YEP. LUCKY YOU.
EXCUSE ME, SIR, HAVE YOU SEEN ANYTHING UNUSUAL AROUND HERE LATELY? MAYBE OBJECTS IN THE SKY OR ANYTHING OF THAT NATURE?
THIS IS UNIT 12. WE'RE AT 23RD AND SEALY. WE'LL TAKE THAT ROBBERY CALL.
SKRTHICT REPEAT,UNIT 12. YOU'RE BREAKING UP.
DUDE, YOU DID NOT SEE A UFO!
I'M TELLING YOU, THEY FLEW RIGHT OVER!
LOUSY RADIOS.
HEY, MAN! YOU'RE KILLING MY BIZ!

WHEEZE
OH MY GOD! I'M GONNA HAVE A HEART ATTACK!
7th Ave
HOUGHTO

NEED TO CUT BACK ON THE PIZZAS!
GASP! *HUNH-HENH*

GREAT. COPS. ALWAYS BUSTING MY CHOPS.

UNIT 12 REQUESTING BACKUP AT --
SQWEEEEE!
FORGET THE RADIO, MORENO, I THINK I CAN HANDLE THIS ONE.

OK, CREEP, PUT THE GUN DOWN! DON'T MAKE THIS DIFFICULT!

DIFFICULT, HUH? I'LL GIVE YOU DIFFICULT!

BLAM! BLAM!

TONK!

TINK-
KRTL-
KRTL

I'M OK, MORENO! HE MISSED!
LUCK!
B-BUT I SAW --
HE'S GETTING AWAY!

MAN! HE'S FAST FOR A BIG GUY!
I'LL NEVER HEAR THE END OF IT FROM MORENO IF HE GETS AWAY THOUGH.

HUNH-
HUNH--

WHEEZE...I... SAID...

STOP!
THIP!

OH, SH----

OOOFFF!
TH-MAK!

COME ON, COME ON -

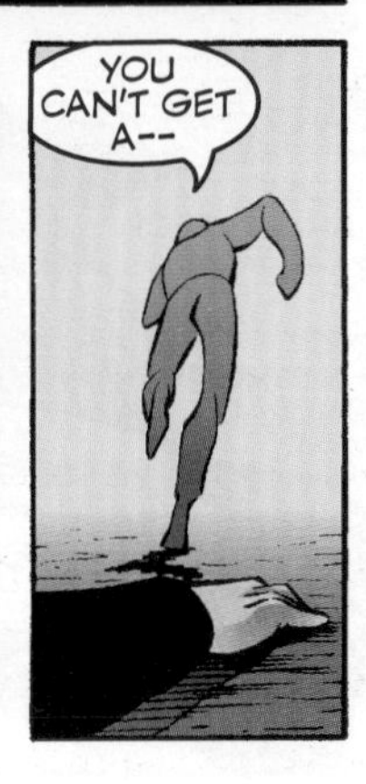
YOU CAN'T GET A--

--WAY?

YOU READY TO GIVE UP NOW?
LUCK! ARE YOU --
GET HIM AWAY FROM ME! HE'S SOME KIND OF FREAK! I SHOT HIM BUT-- GET AWAY!

ARE YOU SURE YOU'RE OK? IT LOOKED LIKE --

WHAT? YOU'RE ACTUALLY WORRIED ABOUT ME? TESS, ARE YOU FEELING OK?

JUST CUFF HIM AND LET'S GO.
AND DON'T CALL ME TESS.

YOU UNDERSTAND THESE RIGHTS I HAVE READ TO YOU?
LISTEN TO ME, LADY! THIS THING SHOT OUT AND TRIPPED ME--
SOME LONG ARM OUT OF HIS CHEST! I SWEAR IT!
I SHOT HIM AND NOTHING HAPPENED! I SWEAR!
SIGH WE'RE GONNA HAVE TO GET MENTAL HEALTH TO COME TAKE A LOOK AT THIS GUY.

YOU GOTTA BELIEVE ME! HE'S SOME KIND OF **FREAK!**

IT'S OK. EVERYTHING'S GOING TO BE JUST FINE. WHEN WE GET TO THE STATION, YOU'LL MEET A NICE DOCTOR. DON'T YOU WORRY.

NO, YOU DON'T UNDERSTAND! HE'S A MONSTER OR ... AN ALIEN!
I BET HE HATCHED OUT OF ONE OF THOSE SPACESHIPS!

THAT'S RIGHT. I'M A CREATURE FROM ANOTHER WORLD, AND IF YOU KEEP TRYING TO EXPOSE ME, I'M GONNA SUCK OUT YOUR BRAIN AND--

THAT'S ENOUGH, LUCK!
I SWEAR, I FEEL MORE LIKE YOUR BABYSITTER THAN YOUR PARTNER!

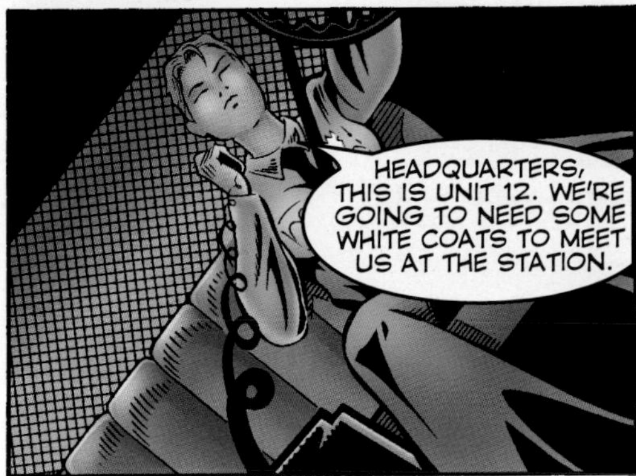
HEADQUARTERS, THIS IS UNIT 12. WE'RE GOING TO NEED SOME WHITE COATS TO MEET US AT THE STATION.

TEN-FOUR, UNIT 12. WE WILL ***SKRICHT*** DOCTOR KO ***RSHTCKT*** ER AND TELL HIM TO MEET Y ***SHRTHEEEEEEE***
WHAT IS WITH ALL THIS RADIO INTERFERENCE?

... ONE OF OUR MEN. SAW IT ALL. DEFINITELY HIM.
YOU IDIOT! IT WAS A SIMPLE HIT!
HOW HARD COULD IT BE?
THAM!
WELL, HE MUST BE DISPOSED OF. WE DON'T KNOW WHAT HE MAY HAVE SEEN. AND WE STILL HAVE MORENO TO TAKE CARE OF.
AND WHAT OF OUR LITTLE ALIEN-FRIEND? ANY SIGN OF HIM?
STILL LOOKING. POSSIBLE SIGHTINGS. NO DEFINITES.
CONTINUE LOOKING. HE IS OF NO USE TO US IF WE DON'T KNOW WHERE HE IS.
IN THE MEANTIME, GET SGT. LIEUTENANT HERE.
YES, SIR. RIGHT AWAY.

6:45 PM
GOOD JOB, LUCK! THAT GUY'S BEEN HITTING FAST-FOOD JOINTS FOR MONTHS!
I'M EVEN WILLING TO FORGET YOU WERE LATE.

DON'T FORGET MY PARTNER, THE LOVELY AND TALENTED TESSA MORENO. SHE WAS INSTRUMENTAL IN ... UH ... DRIVING THE CAR.
CAPTAIN, I'M BEGGING YOU TO ASSIGN ME ANOTHER PARTNER.

LOOK, MORENO, IT'S NOT THAT EASY. WE PUT A LOT OF THOUGHT INTO THESE ASSIGNMENTS, AND --
OH MY GOD, MY TIE! HE BARELY MISSED!
BRRRRRING!
BRRRRR
HOLD THAT THOUGHT. I GOTTA TAKE THIS.

PATROL, TANNER.
WHAT? WHERE?
WHY DIDN'T YOU CALL IT IN?

NO ANSWER? I'LL HAVE SOMEONE OVER THERE. ASAP.

HEY! WHILE YOU TWO ARE CACKLING LIKE TWO HENS, WE HAVE A POSSIBLE WIFE-BEATING AT SOME APARTMENTS ON 51ST!
DISPATCH HAS BEEN TRYING TO REACH YOU TWO FOR 10 MINUTES!
BUT, CAPTAIN, THE RADIOS AREN'T --
I DON'T WANT EXCUSES! I WANT YOU OVER THERE! NOW! APARTMENT 951!

ALL RIGHT. THIS IS IT.

HOW DO YOU WANT TO WORK THIS? JUST WALK IN?
I DON'T WANT TO STAND OUT HERE DISCUSSING IT WHEN WE COULD HAVE A WOMAN IN TROUBLE UP THERE. LET'S GO!

I SURE HOPE THEY'VE GOT AN ELEVATOR.
DO YOU *EVER* STOP TALKING?

SHEESH. WHAT'S YOUR PROBLEM?
ROOKIES.

OOH, TOUCHED A NERVE DID I? YOU HAVE SOME SORT OF VESTED INTEREST HERE? SOMETHING YOU WANT TO TALK ABOUT?
NOT WITH YOU. NOW CLIMB.

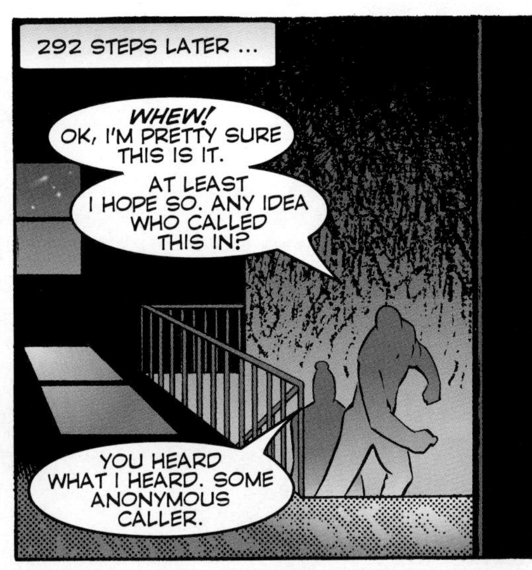
292 STEPS LATER ...
WHEW! OK, I'M PRETTY SURE THIS IS IT.
AT LEAST I HOPE SO. ANY IDEA WHO CALLED THIS IN?
YOU HEARD WHAT I HEARD. SOME ANONYMOUS CALLER.

HERE IT IS - APARTMENT 951.
OH, JUST LET ME GET MY HANDS ON THIS ABUSIVE CREEP, I'LL --

WAIT.

CHECK IT OUT, THE DOOR'S ALREADY PARTIALLY OPEN.

YOU OK, MORENO? YOU LOOK A LITTLE DISTURBED.
YEAH, I'M FINE. NOW LET'S GET THIS OVER WITH.

OK, THIS IS THE POLICE! WHAT SEEMS TO BE THE PROBLEM?

HOW MANY TIMES DO I HAVE TO TELL YOU, WOMAN?! WHEN I GET HOME, I EXPECT A GOOD MEAL READY!
HUNH? WHAT DO YOU WANT?

YOU THINK YOU CAN JUST COME BUSTIN' IN HERE WHEN I'M HAVING A TALK WITH MY OLD LADY?
SIR, I SUGGEST YOU...
...CALM DOWN.
K-DONK!
OOOFFF!
SO YOU WANT TO PLAY ROUGH?
COME ON LUCK, YOU GET HIM. YOU WANNA BE ROOKIE OF THE YEAR, RIGHT?
NO PROBLEM. I'LL, UH --
UH-OH.

OFFICER ... LUCK, IS IT? METHANE SAID TO TELL YOU HELLO.
UUNHH!
AND NOW, I'M GONNA FINISH THE JOB HE STARTED!
WOK!

KRAAK!

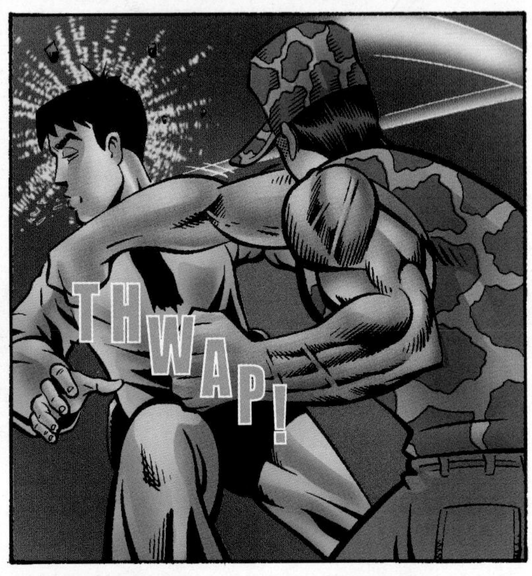
THWAP!

DANG.

WHAM!

KRRASH!

!HHHAAAA
PLEASE LET THIS BE ANOTHER NIGHTMARE!

WHAT THE...
I DON'T BELIEVE THIS...
BUT HOW...
LUCK! NO!
STAY HERE, MA'AM, I'VE GOT TO CHECK ON MY PARTNER! DON'T WORRY! HE'S NOT GOING TO HURT YOU ANYMORE!
WELL, HONEY, THAT'S ONE WAY OF PUTTIN' IT ...
?!

Y'SEE, I'M WHATCHA MIGHT CALL ...
... NOT AS FRAIL ...
... AS MY GOILISH FIG-YAH MIGHT LEAD YA TA B'LIEVE!
AN' NOW, WE'RE GONNA SETTLE THIS WOMAN TO WOMAN, LIKE!
HEH-HEH-HEH.
TH-MAAK!

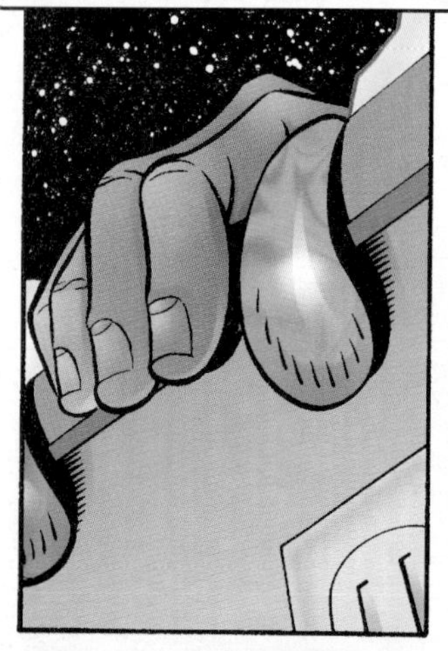
IN LESS THAN TWO DAYS
I HAD ESCAPED DEATH TWICE.

TWO
CAN PLAY AT THAT
GAME!

WA-POW!

WUSS.

WH
OP!

?

...OR
NOT.

TO BE CONTINUED!

Alternate Cover Image by Courtney Huddleston and Bob Almond

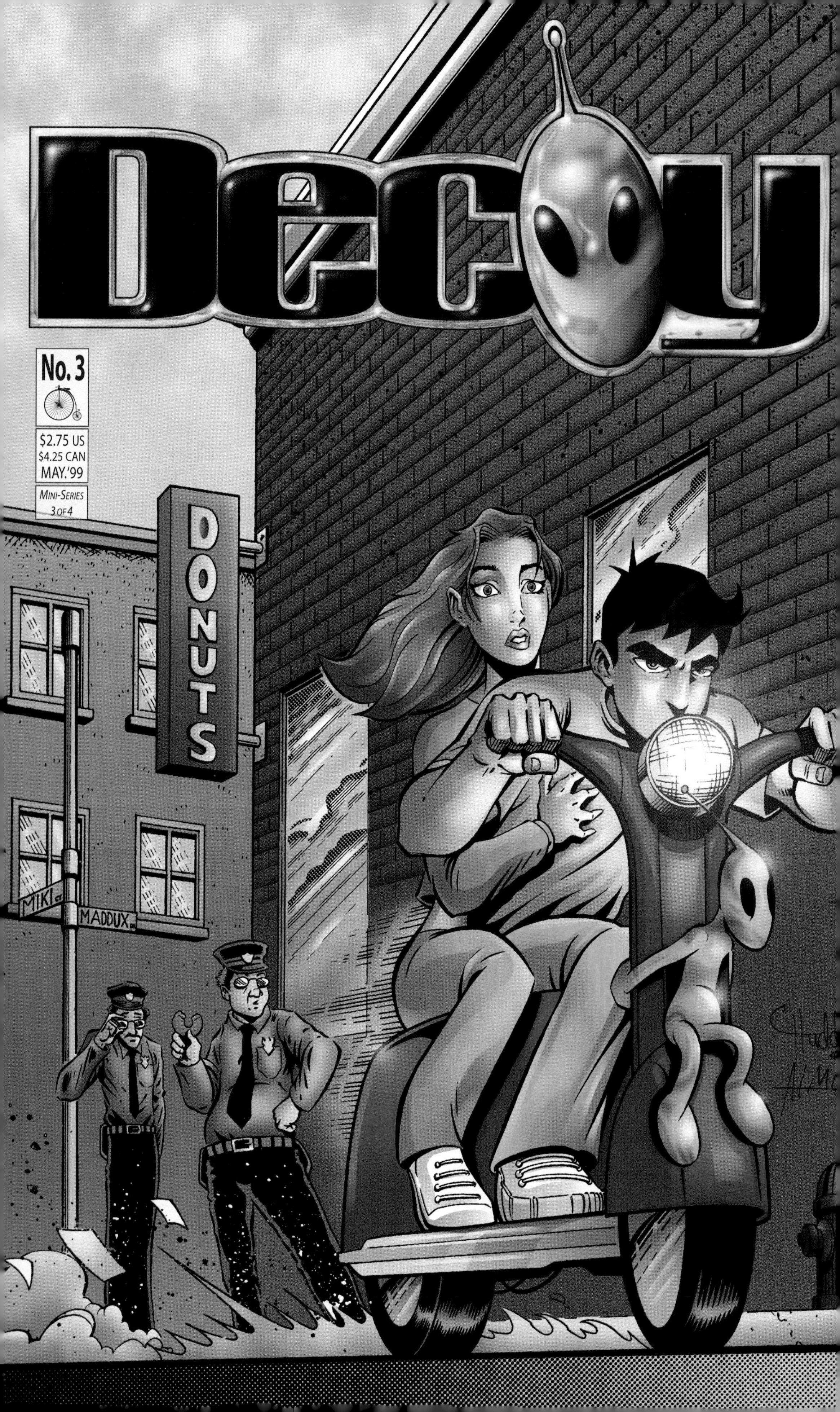
Decoy
No. 3
$2.75 US
$4.25 CAN
MAY.'99
Mini-Series
3 of 4
DONUTS
MIKI
MADDUX

DOLPHIN CITY IS FAMOUS THROUGHOUT THE REGION FOR ITS BEAUTIFUL, PEACEFUL NIGHTS.
NORMALLY I HELP KEEP THAT PEACE, BUT TONIGHT...
AAAAAAAAHHHHHHHH!
UHHH...
AHHH...
AAAAHHHHH

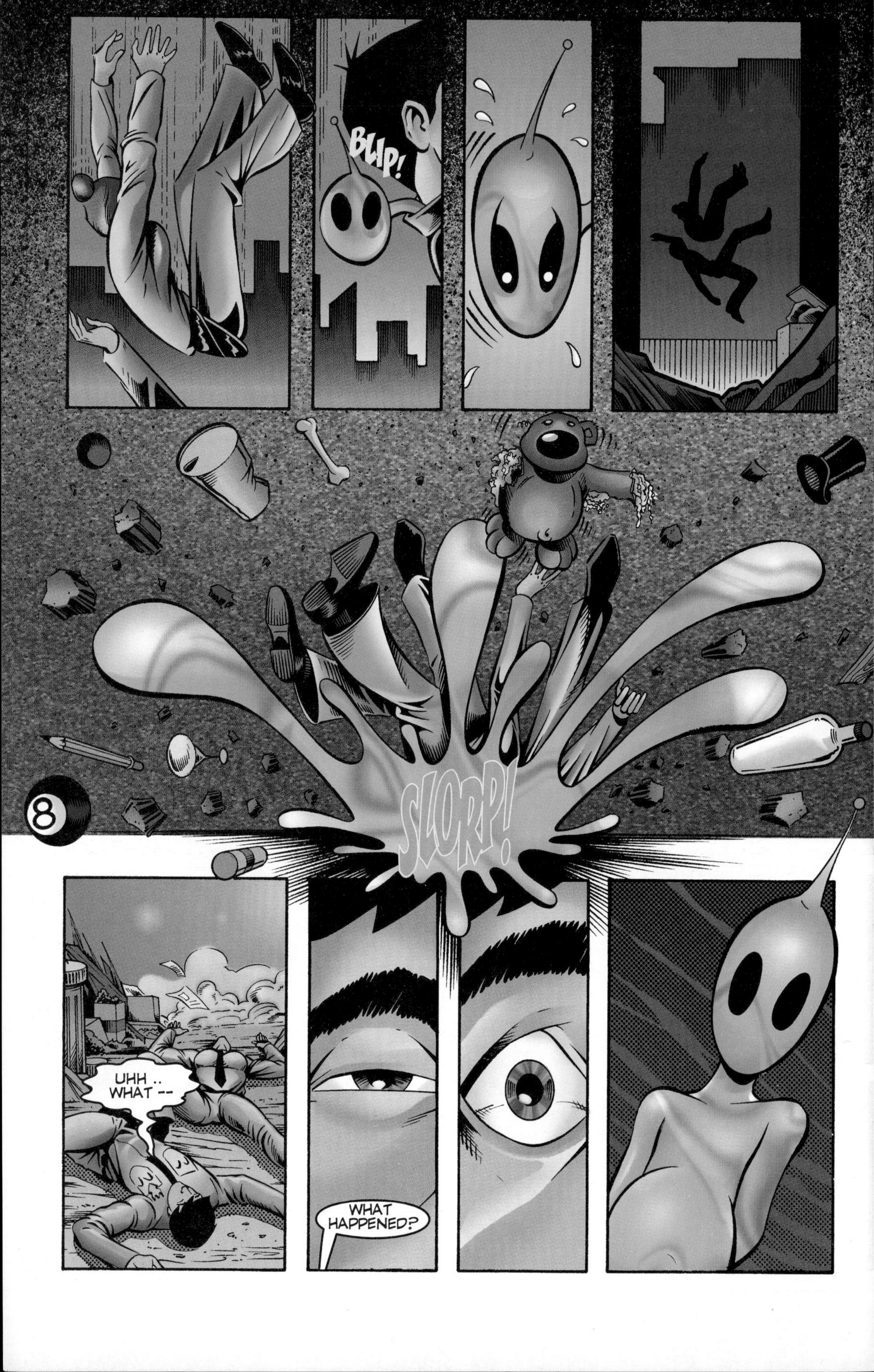
BLIP!
SLORP!
UHH .. WHAT --
WHAT HAPPENED?

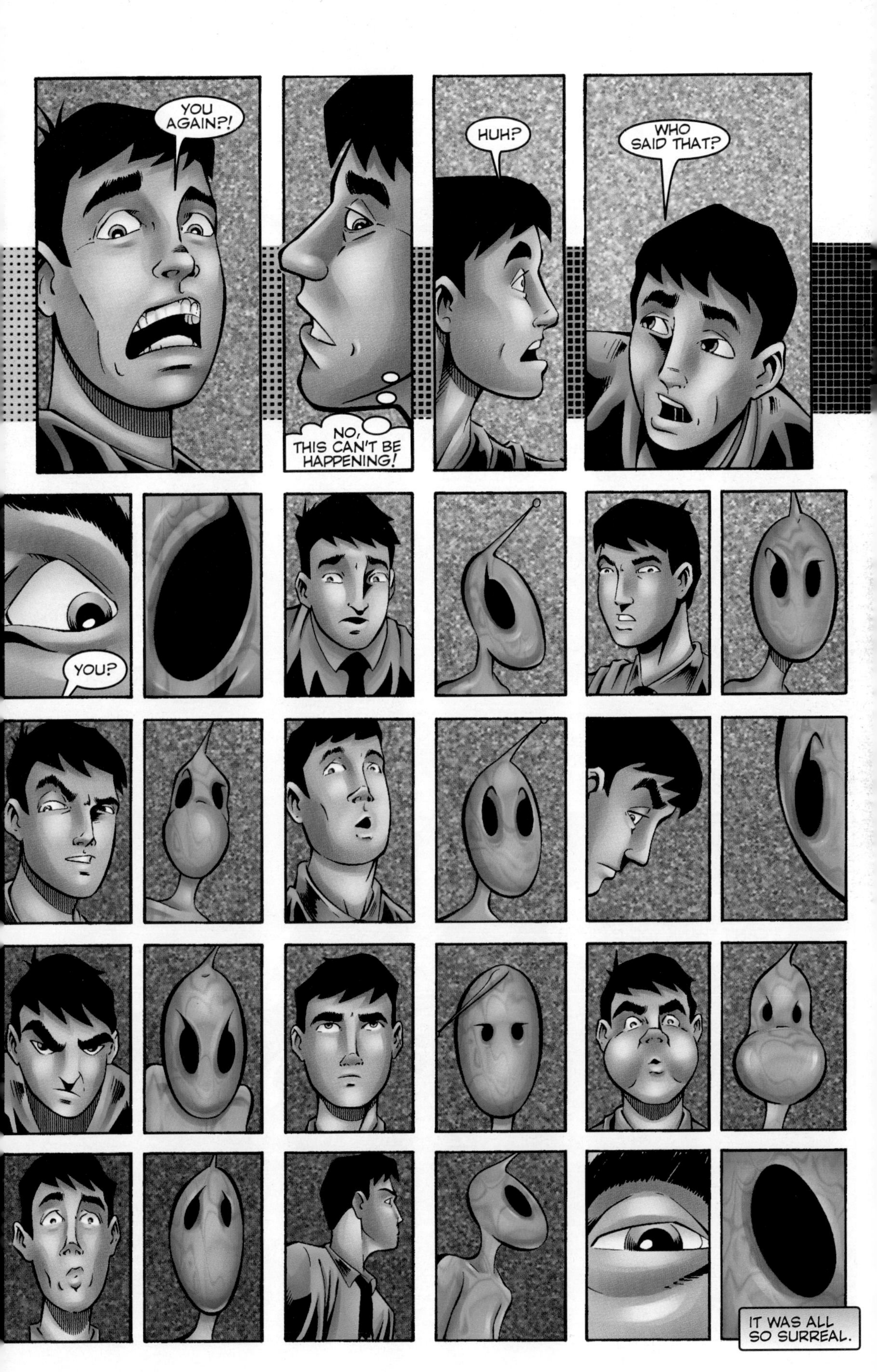
YOU AGAIN?!
NO, THIS CAN'T BE HAPPENING!
HUH?
WHO SAID THAT?
YOU?
IT WAS ALL SO SURREAL.

AND YET, I BARELY QUESTIONED ANY OF IT.
... LET ME MAKE SURE I'VE GOT THIS STRAIGHT.
YOU CAME FROM ANOTHER PLANET, CHASING AN ESCAPED PRISONER, BUT YOUR COMRADES LEFT YOU BEHIND AFTER YOU OBJECTED TO THEIR CRUEL TREATMENT OF SAID PRISONER, THE KRANCH, OR WHATEVER YOU CALLED HIM.
SO, I **WAS** IN THE WOODS, THAT MASKED MANIAC **DID** SHOOT ME, THEN YOU FOUND ME AND ... BROUGHT ME BACK TO LIFE BY FILLING MY WOUNDS WITH YOUR ... YOUR ... ALIEN POWER OR WHATEVER?
AND NOW WE SHARE A TELEPATHIC BOND, AND WE ARE, FOR ALL INTENTS AND PURPOSES, STUCK WITH EACH OTHER. AM I GETTING IT RIGHT SO FAR?
BUT WHY?
WHY HELP ME, WHEN YOU KNEW DOING IT WOULD STRAND YOU HERE FOREVER?
WHAT DO YOU MEAN, "NOT ACCEPTED?" YOU SEEM HARMLESS ENOUGH TO ME. OH--THAT'S THE PROBLEM.
WELL, LET ME TELL YOU, I CAN'T THANK YOU ENOUGH FOR SAVING MY...
SO WAIT A MINUTE--YOU SAID YOU CAN CHANGE YOUR SHAPE?
INTO ANYTHING?

NOT BAD, NOT BAD. HERE -- TRY THIS ONE.

NO, YOU'RE NOT. YOU'RE BIG-BONED. HOW ABOUT --

NOW A REAL BEAR.

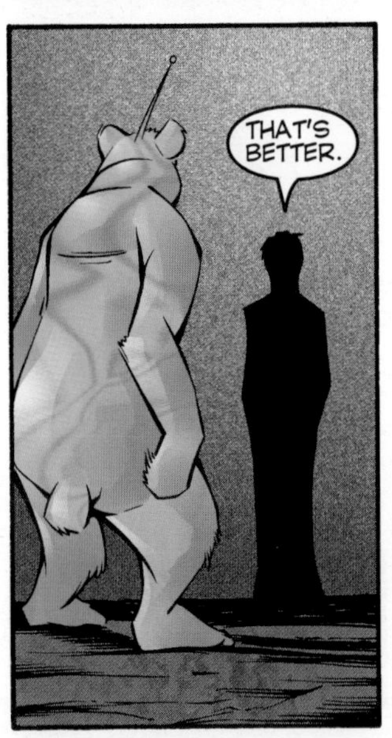
THAT'S BETTER.

WHOA -- YOU'RE HOLLOW! COOL!
THOM-THOM

OKAY, TRY...

A SPY.

A DETECTIVE.

A HAMBURGER. HA!
MILK

WHAT?
OH, TESSA!

OHHH ... WHAT HAPPENED? DID WE GET THE GUY --

LUCK? HOW DID WE --

I MEAN, WE FELL -
OKAY, CALM DOWN. IT WAS, UH, OUR FRIENDLY NEIGHBORHOOD SP...

YEAH, RIGHT.

SERIOUSLY THOUGH...
QUICK, SHE'LL FREAK OUT IF SHE SEES YOU, TURN INTO SOMETHING ELSE -- I'LL COME BACK FOR YOU.

HURRY UP! SHE'S GONNA SEE YOU!
LUCK! ARE YOU LISTENING?!

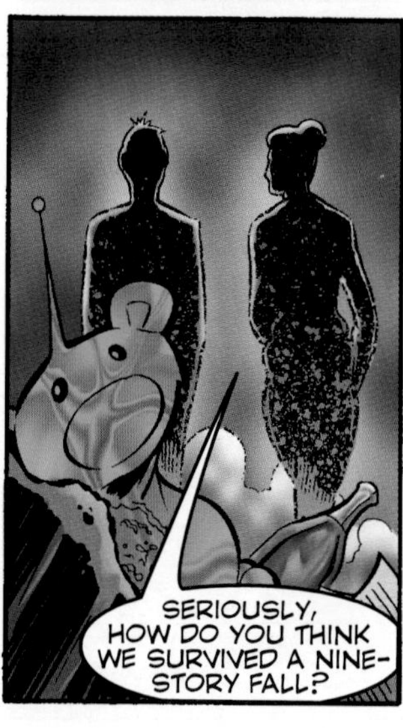
SERIOUSLY, HOW DO YOU THINK WE SURVIVED A NINE-STORY FALL?

WEEE-OOOOO
WEEE-OOOOO
SCRREECH
THERE THEY ARE!
MAN, I HOPE THEY'RE OK!!
HEY, YOU GUYS AREN'THURT! WE GOT A CALL FROM A LADY ACROSS THE STREET SAYING YOU FELL AT LEAST SIX STORIES.
NINE, ACTUALLY.
YEAH. WE'D HAVE BEEN HERE SOONER, BUT OUR RADIOS WOULDN'T PICK UP THE CALL. PIECES OF JUNK. I'LL BE GLAD WHEN WE GET THOSE NEW SYSTEMS.

EITHER ONE OF YOU TWO SEE ANYONE COME OUT OF THE BUILDING?

NO ONE SAW ANYONE COME OUT. IN FACT, THAT WHOLE BUILDING'S BEEN CONDEMNED FOR MONTHS. NO ONE LIVES THERE.
C'MON, MORENO, YOU LOOK PRETTY SHAKY. LET'S LET THE E.M.S. CREW TAKE A LOOK AT YOU.

YOU KNOW HOW I WORRY ABOUT YOU.
YEAH, I KNOW HOW YOU WORRY I'M GONNA MAKE SERGEANT BEFORE YOU, NEWSOM. YOU COMING, LUCK?
I'LL BE RIGHT THERE. I ... THINK I DROPPED SOMETHING.

A THING OF BEAUTY.
DOCTOR! HAVE YOU SUCCESSFULLY COMPLETED THE REWIRING OF THE DEVICE?
ALMOST, SIR. I'VE GOT ONE LAST KINK TO WORK OUT ...
... AND IT SHOULD PERFORM PERFECTLY! GIVE ME 24 HOURS, AND THE CITY WILL BE OURS!

FOOL! I TOLD YOU BY DAWN! AND THE CITY WILL BE MINE, ALONE.

YOU ARE ***NOBODY*** HERE--NOTHING MORE THAN A PAWN, A MECHANIC, AND NOT A VERY GOOD ONE AT THAT. WHERE I COME FROM YOU WOULD HAVE BEEN ***DESTROYED*** FOR YOUR INCOMPETENCE LONG AGO.

NOW, HERE'S THE PRESS RELEASE. SEE TO ITS EXECUTION IMMEDIATELY.
DO NOT FAIL.
YES SIR, I UNDERSTAND SIR.

"...WITH THE PUSH OF A BUTTON ..."
WITH THE PUSH OF A BUTTON INDEED.

10:05
...WITH THE PUSH OF A BUTTON, DOLPHIN CITY'S FINEST WILL BE READY TO MOVE INTO THE 21ST CENTURY WITH A FUTURISTIC COMMUNICATIONS SYSTEM TO REPLACE THE CURRENT POLICE RADIOS.
SO HOW MANY TIMES, EXACTLY, *HAVE* YOU SAVED ME? THREE, FOUR, FIVE? I MEAN, THE FALLS...AND ALL THOSE *BULLETS!* HOW'D YOU DO THAT?

A SHIELD-- YOU *SHIELDED* ME? BUT I DIDN'T FEEL THE BULLET HIT AT ALL!

WOW! TO THINK I SHOULD'VE BEEN DEAD A LONG TIME AGO IF YOU HADN'T COME ALONG.

WHAT'S YOUR NAME ANYWAY?

WHAT THE *HECK* DID YOU JUST SAY?

HOLD THAT THOUGHT. I WANT TO HEAR THIS.
THE FUNTECH CORPORATION IS HOLDING A PRESS CONFERENCE TOMORROW MORNING TO ANNOUNCE THE DEVELOPMENT OF A NEW, MORE EFFICIENT POLICE RADIO SYSTEM...

FUNTECH VICE-PRESIDENT JIM WATERSON WILL BE ON HAND TO ACTIVATE THE NEW SYSTEM --

HEY! THAT'S THAT GUY!

WHAT AM I GOING TO DO? I CAN'T GO THROUGH WITH THIS, BUT IF I REFUSE NABOB WILL...

BLING-BOONG
OH NO!

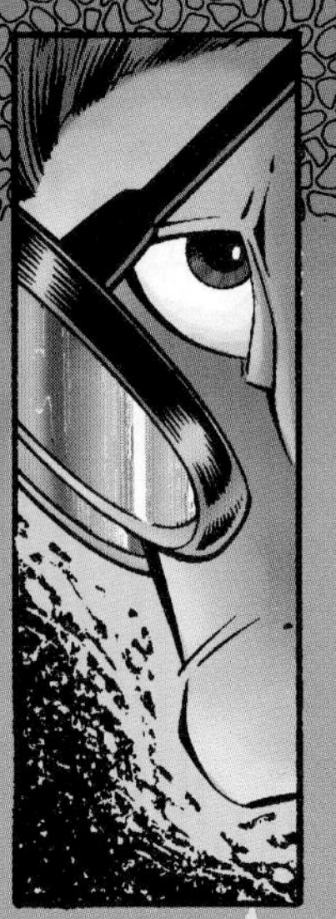

WHA-- YOU?

SURPRISED TO SEE ME? I GUESS SO, SINCE WHEN WE LAST PARTED, I WAS LAID OUT WITH A BULLET IN ME.
MIND IF I COME IN?

DO I HAVE MUCH OF A CHOICE? HOW DID YOU FIND ME?

A LITTLE ADVICE -- IF YOU DON'T WANT TO BE FOUND, KEEP YOUR FACE OFF TV AND GET AN UNLISTED NUMBER AND ADDRESS. BESIDES, IT'S WHAT I DO.

NICE PLACE.
THANKS. NOW, WHAT IS IT YOU WANT?

WHAT DO I WANT?!

YOU LEFT ME FOR DEAD! WHAT I WANT IS TO KICK YOUR TEETH IN! AND THAT MAY BE EXACTLY WHAT I DO UNLESS YOU START TELLING ME WHAT'S GOING ON

I CAN'T -- I, THAT IS, THEY WILL -- I --

LET'S SEE... HOW CAN I MAKE THIS EASIER FOR YOU? DOES JAIL SOUND GOOD?

NO, YOU DON'T UNDERSTAND! PLEASE!

YEAH, OBSTRUCTION OF JUSTICE AND CONSORTING WITH KNOWN CRIMINALS. THAT SHOULD GET YOU A FEW YEARS.

OKAY, OKAY, BUT... NOT HERE. IT'S TOO RISKY.

WHY DON'T WE TAKE A WALK.

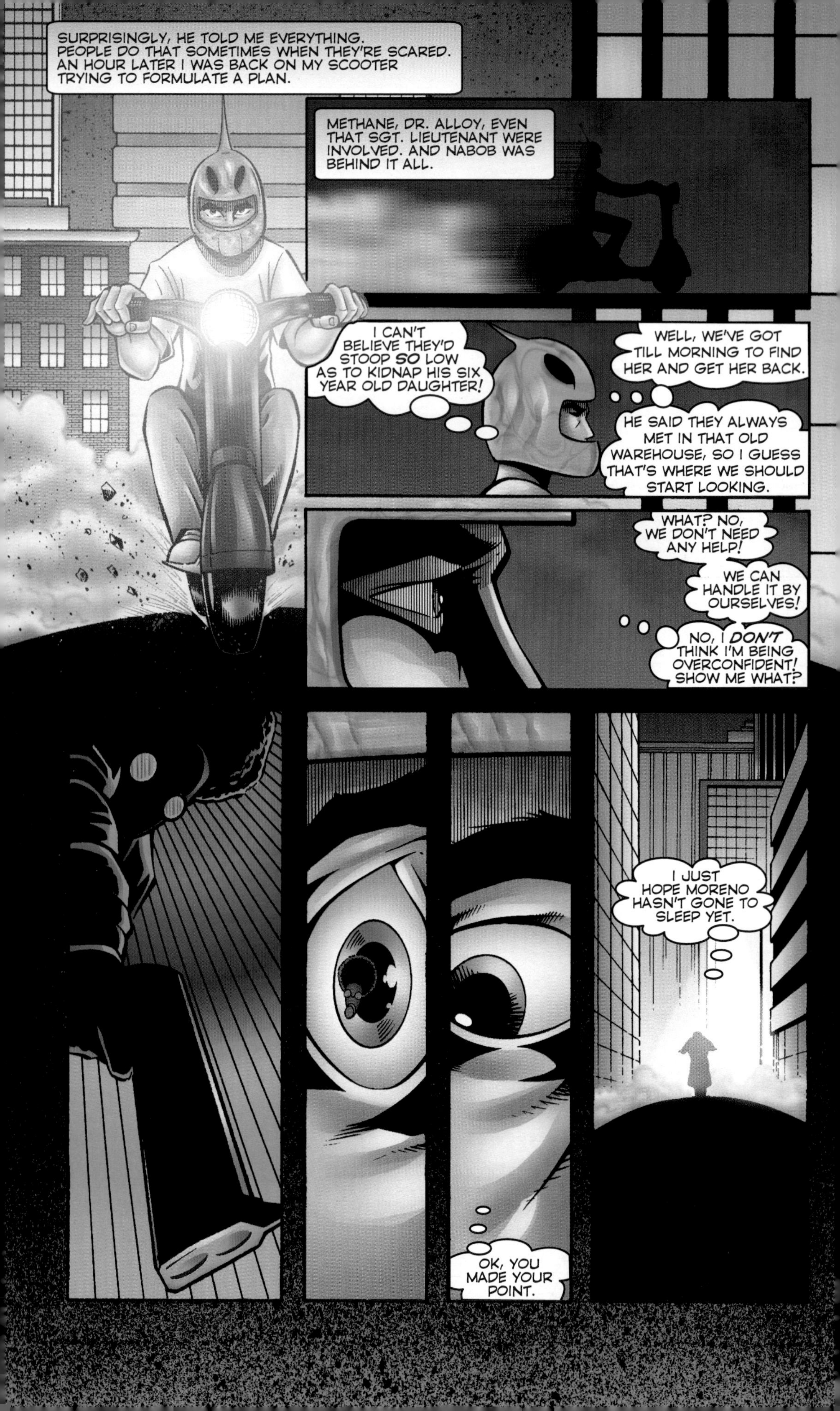
SURPRISINGLY, HE TOLD ME EVERYTHING. PEOPLE DO THAT SOMETIMES WHEN THEY'RE SCARED. AN HOUR LATER I WAS BACK ON MY SCOOTER TRYING TO FORMULATE A PLAN.
METHANE, DR. ALLOY, EVEN THAT SGT. LIEUTENANT WERE INVOLVED. AND NABOB WAS BEHIND IT ALL.
I CAN'T BELIEVE THEY'D STOOP SO LOW AS TO KIDNAP HIS SIX YEAR OLD DAUGHTER!
WELL, WE'VE GOT TILL MORNING TO FIND HER AND GET HER BACK.
HE SAID THEY ALWAYS MET IN THAT OLD WAREHOUSE, SO I GUESS THAT'S WHERE WE SHOULD START LOOKING.
WHAT? NO, WE DON'T NEED ANY HELP!
WE CAN HANDLE IT BY OURSELVES!
NO, I DON'T THINK I'M BEING OVERCONFIDENT! SHOW ME WHAT?
OK, YOU MADE YOUR POINT.
I JUST HOPE MORENO HASN'T GONE TO SLEEP YET.

THIS HAD BETTER BE GOOD, LUCK! WHAT IS SO IMPORTANT THAT IT CAN'T WAIT UNTIL MORNING?
RRRRRRRRRRRRRRRR
YOU KNOW THOSE NEW RADIOS WE'RE GETTING TOMORROW?

THEY'RE BOMBS.
WHAT?!
RRRRR

WATERSON'S DAUGHTER WAS KIDNAPPED. AND UNLESS HE INSTALLED THESE EXPLOSIVE DEVICES IN THE RADIOS HIS COMPANY'S MAKING FOR US, THE KIDNAPPERS THREATENED TO KILL BOTH HIM AND HIS DAUGHTER.
WHY? WHO ARE THE KIDNAPPERS?
NABOB GANG.

HAVE YOU TOLD ANY OF THIS TO TANNER?
NO, HE WOULDN'T TAKE MY CALL--TOO BUSY ON SOME TIP.
RRRRR

WHICH MEANS-- HE CAN'T SLOW US DOWN!
WELL, AT THIS RATE WE'RE NEVER GOING TO GET ANYWHERE! MY CAR GOES FASTER THAN THIS WHEN IT'S PARKED!

CLICK!
IF IT'S SPEED YOU WANT ...

Luck,
if you kill me,
I swear I'll come
back and kick your
aaaaaahhhhhhh!!!
@!?*

CUT
ME OFF, YOU
@!%*!

WHOA.

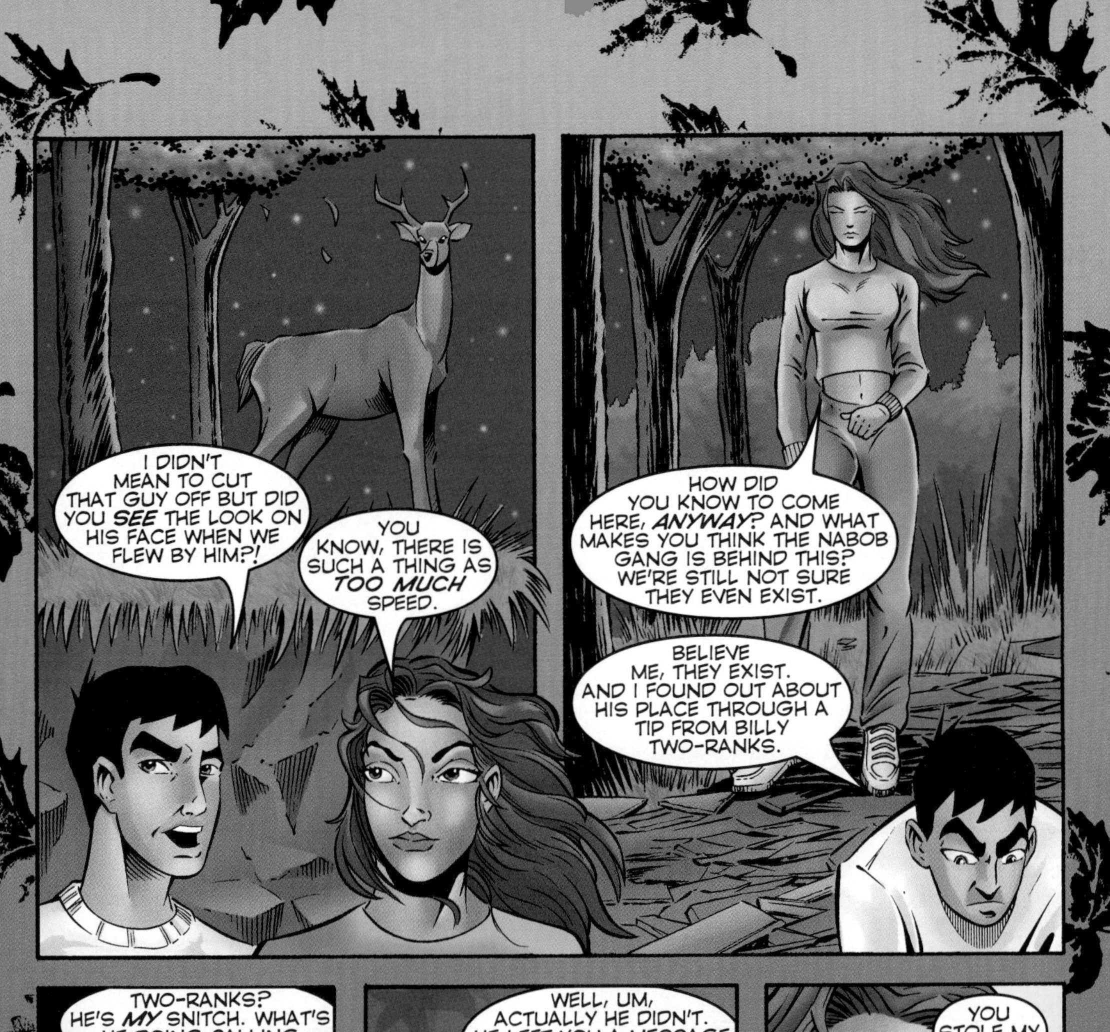
I DIDN'T MEAN TO CUT THAT GUY OFF BUT DID YOU SEE THE LOOK ON HIS FACE WHEN WE FLEW BY HIM?!
YOU KNOW, THERE IS SUCH A THING AS TOO MUCH SPEED.
HOW DID YOU KNOW TO COME HERE, ANYWAY? AND WHAT MAKES YOU THINK THE NABOB GANG IS BEHIND THIS? WE'RE STILL NOT SURE THEY EVEN EXIST.
BELIEVE ME, THEY EXIST. AND I FOUND OUT ABOUT HIS PLACE THROUGH A TIP FROM BILLY TWO-RANKS.

TWO-RANKS? HE'S MY SNITCH. WHAT'S HE DOING CALLING YOU?

WELL, UM, ACTUALLY HE DIDN'T. HE LEFT YOU A MESSAGE ABOUT THIS PLACE, AND I FOLLOWED UP ON IT.

YOU STOLE MY TIP?

I KNOW. IT WAS A LOUSY THING TO DO, BUT NOW'S NOT THE TIME. WE'VE GOT A LITTLE GIRL THAT NEEDS SAVING.

FINE, BUT DON'T THINK I'LL FORGET THIS.

LET'S GO. I THINK I KNOW WHERE THEY ARE!

LATER.
YOU WANT TO TELL ME WHY WE'RE AT THE N.W.O.T. BUILDING NOW?
THE PAPER I FOUND IN THE WRECKAGE-- IT WAS THEIR LETTERHEAD.
SO?
WHAT MAKES YOU THINK SHE'S HERE?
IT'S ALL WE'VE GOT! YOU HAVE ANY BETTER IDEAS?
NOW, KEEP A LOOKOUT WHILE I PICK THIS LOCK.
I CAN'T BELIEVE I'M DOING THIS!
LUCK! THIS IS BREAKING AND ENTERING--WE DON'T HAVE A SEARCH WARRANT! WE'RE RISKING OUR JOBS AND OUR LIVES FOR SOMEONE WE DON'T EVEN KNOW IS HERE! I MEAN, THAT LETTERHEAD COULD'VE BEEN FOR ANYTHING!
SHHHH!
OKAY, FINE. THEN WHAT'S YOUR PLAN?
PLAN?
YEAH, YOU KNOW, LIKE, KIDNAPPERS USUALLY HAVE GUNS AND WE DON'T. SO WHAT ARE WE GOING TO DO?
SHHHH! DID YOU HEAR THAT?

YOU GO ON AHEAD. I'LL CATCH UP.

GO AWAY. I WANT MY DADDY!

SHHH, DON'T BE AFRAID. I'M A POLICE OFFICER.
IS YOUR NAME ASHLEY?

I'M HERE TO HELP YOU.

MY NAME IS BOBBY LUCK. WE'RE GONNA GET YOU OUT OF HERE AND BACK HOME TO YOUR DADDY, OKAY?

OKAY.

HELLO AGAIN, OFFICER LUCK.

HELLO TO YOU TOO!

NNUHHH!
THAK!

LUCK! GET HER OUT OF HERE!

I'VE GOT HER!

YOU DO PRETTY GOOD WHEN HITTING SOMEONE FROM *BEHIND*! I TOOK YOU DOWN BEFORE LITTLE GIRL-- LET'S SEE YOU TRY THAT AGAIN NOW THAT I'M READY FOR YOU.

WELL, DON'T GET YOUR UNDEROOS IN A KNOT, BOY SCOUT.
I MEAN, IT SEEMED ONLY FAIR CONSIDERING YOU DID IT TO ME LAST NIGHT.
DOESN'T PAYBACK JUST SUCK!

NICE. BUT YOU'RE STILL JUST A LITTLE GIRL.

DEAD END, HUH?

OH, THIS IS JUST GETTING BETTER AND BETTER.

STAY BACK HERE ASHLEY. I'LL GET US OUT OF THIS.

WHERE'S MORENO?

GONE.
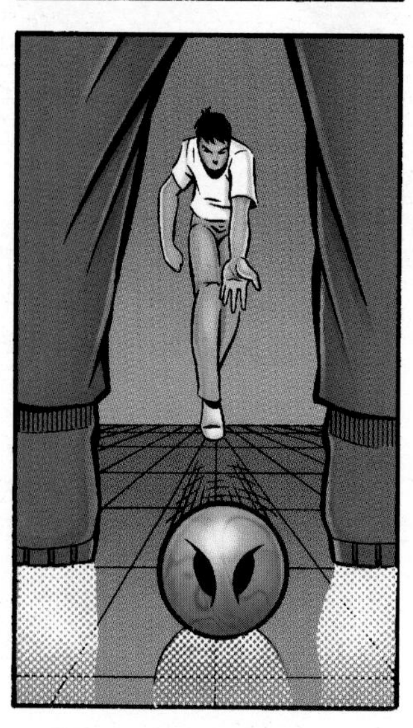
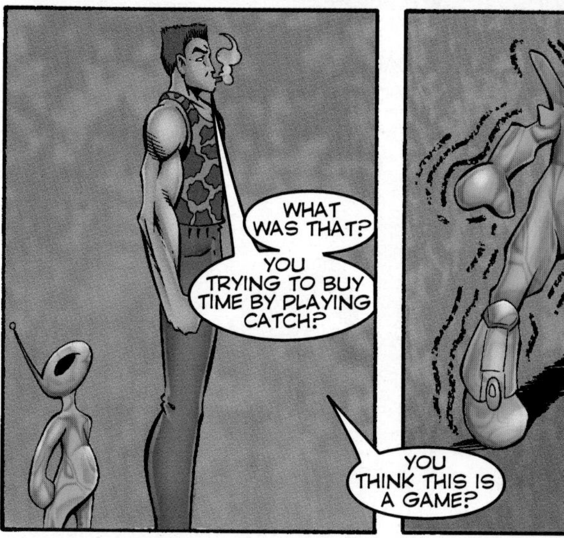
WHAT WAS THAT?
YOU TRYING TO BUY TIME BY PLAYING CATCH?
YOU THINK THIS IS A GAME?

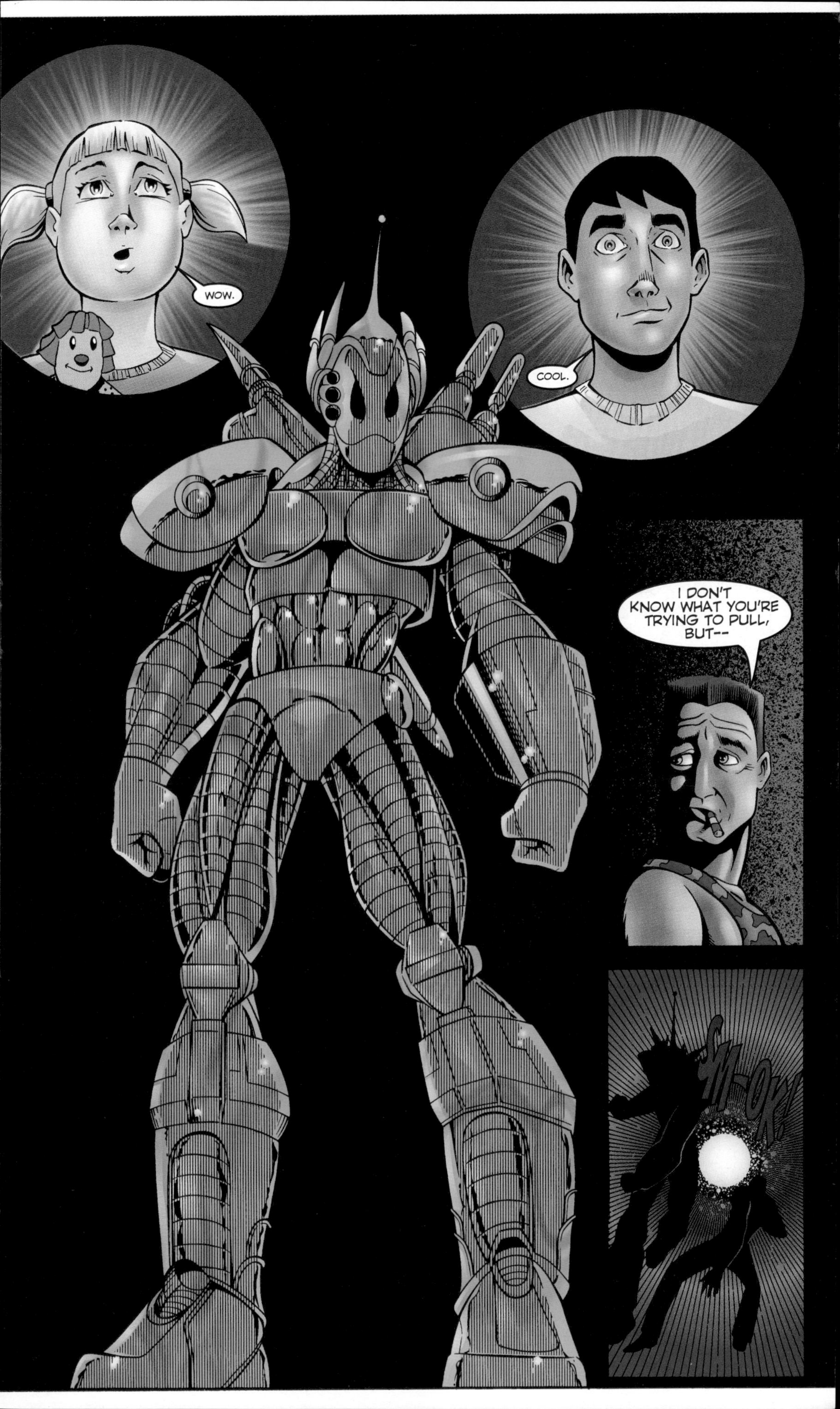
WOW.
COOL.
I DON'T KNOW WHAT YOU'RE TRYING TO PULL, BUT--
SM-OK!

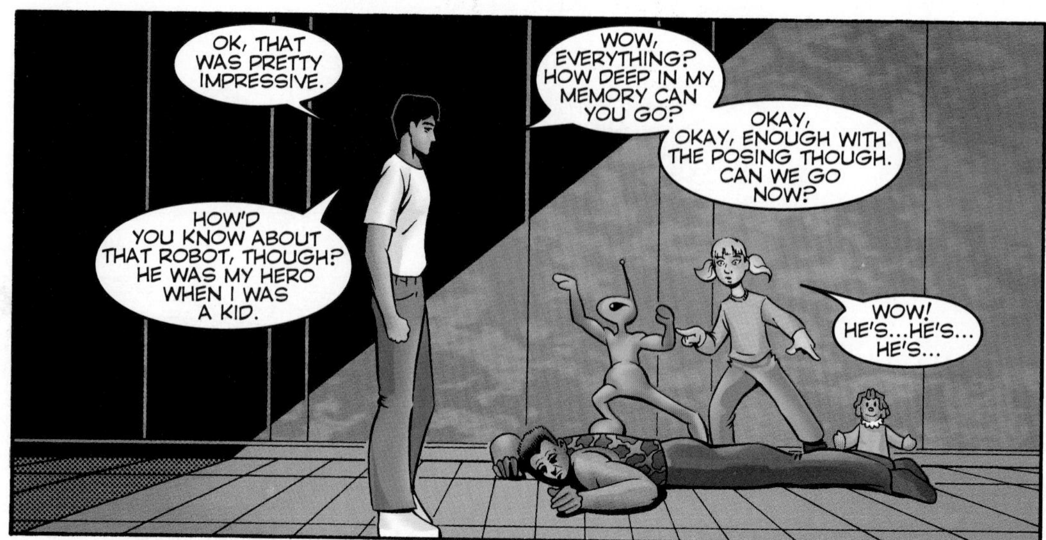
OK, THAT WAS PRETTY IMPRESSIVE.
WOW, EVERYTHING? HOW DEEP IN MY MEMORY CAN YOU GO?
HOW'D YOU KNOW ABOUT THAT ROBOT, THOUGH? HE WAS MY HERO WHEN I WAS A KID.
OKAY, OKAY, ENOUGH WITH THE POSING THOUGH. CAN WE GO NOW?
WOW! HE'S...HE'S... HE'S...

...SOOO CUTE!
CAN I KEEP HIM?

HA, HA! IF YOU TAKE HIM, YOU GOTTA TAKE ME, 'CAUSE WE'RE KINDA INSEPERABLE.

C'MON LITTLE GUY, LET'S GO FIND TESSA AND GET OUTTA HERE.

LET'S GET YOU HOME TO YOUR DAD.

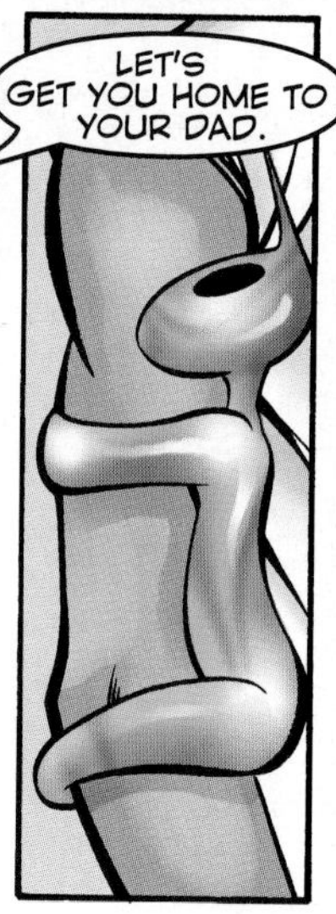

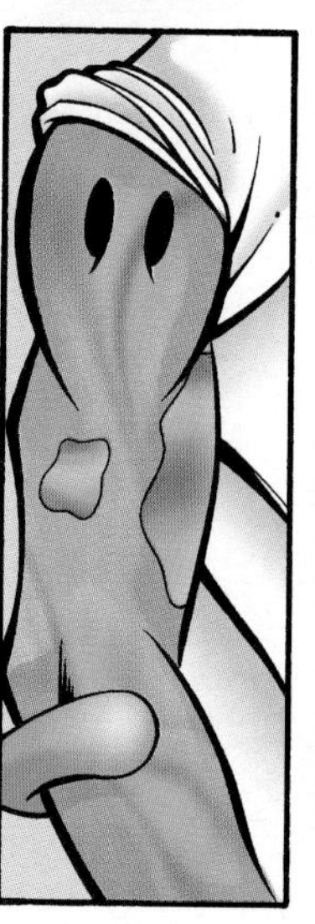

ASHLEY! LOOK OUT!
COUGH, COUGH! WHERE ARE YOU? COUGH!
I CAN'T BREATHE!

WE'RE LESS THAN AN HOUR AWAY FROM THE LONG AWAITED ACTIVATION OF DOLPHIN CITY'S NEW POLICE COMMUNICATION SYSTEM. JOIN US HERE ON CHANNEL 4 AS JIM WATERSON LAUNCHES US INTO THE NEXT PHASE OF CRIME PREVENTION.
TO BE CONTINUED...

Art by Jamal Igle and Bob Waichek

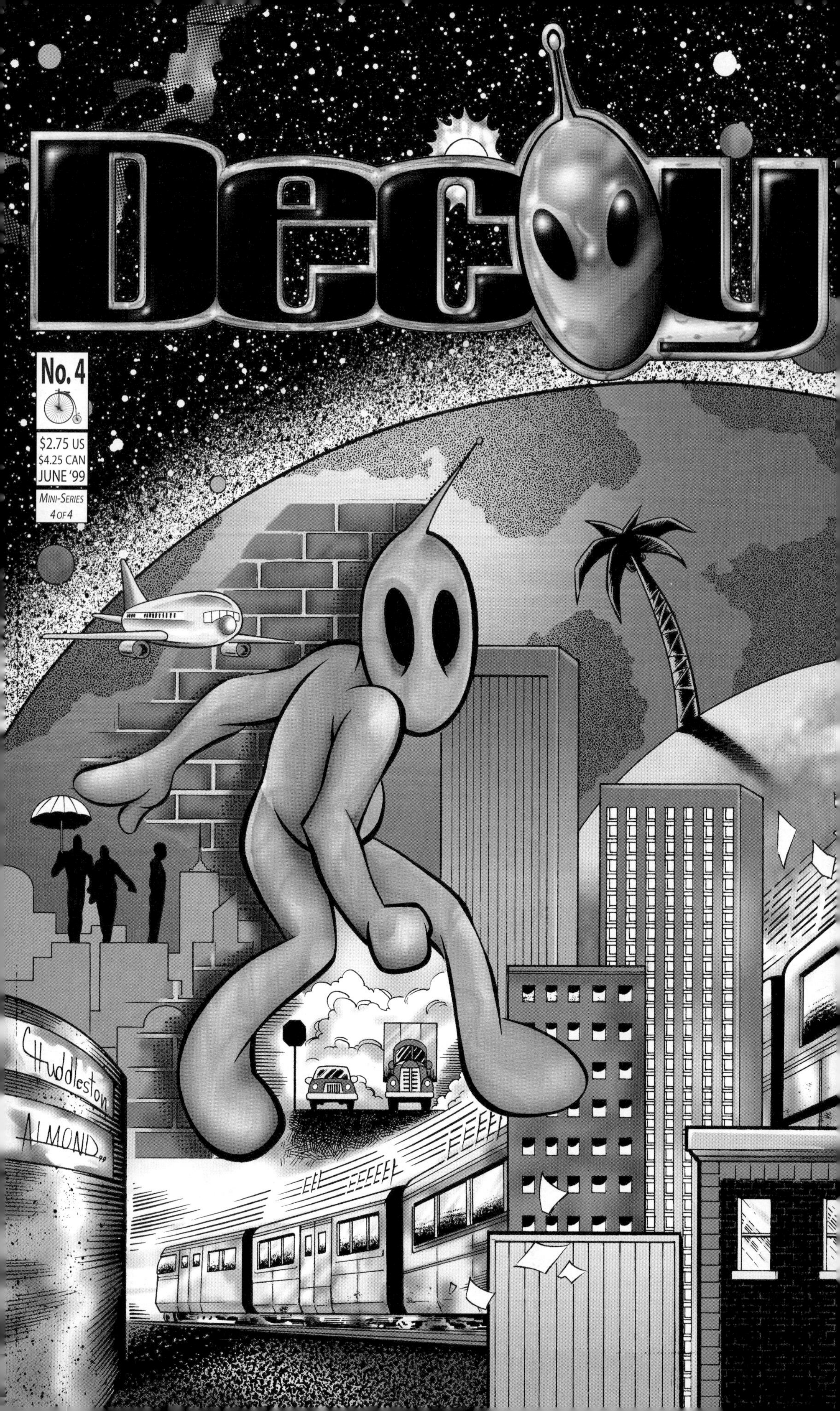
Decoy
No. 4
$2.75 US
$4.25 CAN
JUNE '99
MINI-SERIES
4 OF 4
CHuddleston
ALMOND

AT FIRST, MY WHOLE BODY WAS NUMB.
NABOB, SIR, YOU'RE A VERY BUSY MAN. YOU DON'T NEED TO WASTE YOUR VALUABLE TIME ON A MERE DETAIL LIKE THIS BOY.
THEN I GOT MY HEARING BACK...
THEN MY SIGHT...
I'D BE MORE THAN HAPPY TO DISPOSE OF HIM MYSELF. HIS BODY WOULD BE MOST VALUABLE FOR MY RESEARCH AND...
NO! HE'S MINE!
SILENCE! BOTH OF YOU!
WE HAVE OTHER MATTERS TO ATTEND TO FIRST. DON'T WE, OFFICER LUCK?
AND THEN I REALIZED JUST HOW MUCH THE SITUATION SUCKED.

I DON'T KNOW WHAT YOU'RE TALKING ABOUT, AND EVEN IF I DID, I WOULDN'T GIVE YOU THE PLEASURE. NOW LET ME DOWN!
IN TIME. WHEN YOU GIVE ME WHAT I WANT, I'LL GIVE YOU WHAT YOU WANT.
FIRST THINGS FIRST, THOUGH. METHANE, GO TAKE CARE OF WATERSON. MAKE SURE HE KEEPS HIS END OF OUR LITTLE DEAL. IF NOT, KILL HIM.
NOW, AS I WAS SAYING...

LITTLE META! COME OUT AND SHOW YOURSELF!

UH-OH.

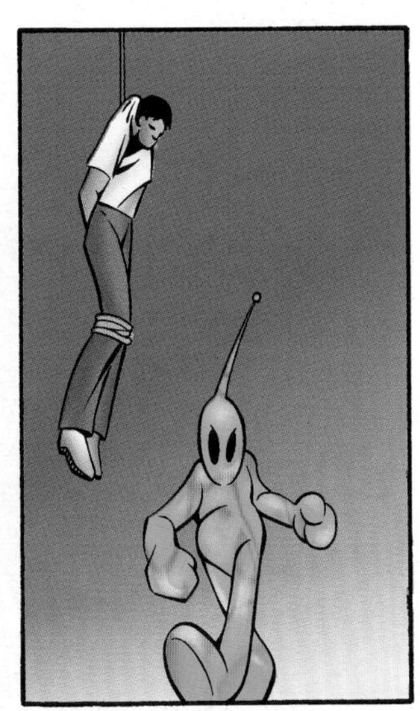

DON'T DO ANYTHING STUPID, *GREEN*. YOU'VE ALREADY COME CLOSE ENOUGH TO RUINING MY PLANS.
I HAD WONDERED WHERE YOU WENT, UNTIL METHANE AND SGT. LIEUTENANT TOLD ME WHAT HAPPENED WHEN THEY EACH CAME IN CONTACT WITH YOUR FRIEND THERE.

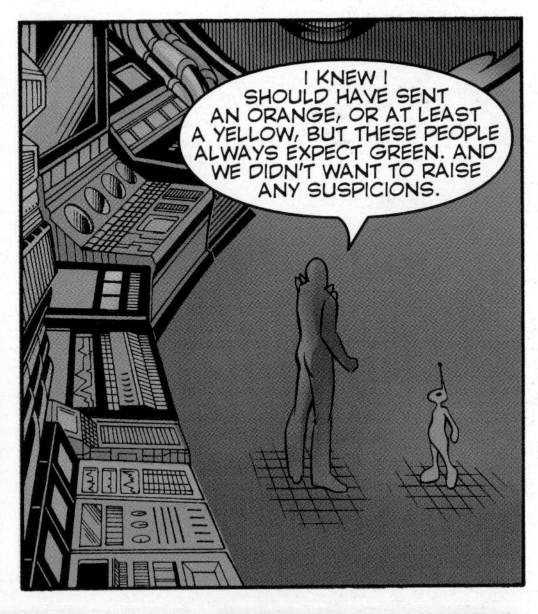
I KNEW I SHOULD HAVE SENT AN ORANGE, OR AT LEAST A YELLOW, BUT THESE PEOPLE ALWAYS EXPECT GREEN. AND WE DIDN'T WANT TO RAISE ANY SUSPICIONS.

ALL YOU HAD TO DO WAS KEEP THEM BUSY--TIE THEM UP--CONFUSE THEM.
THAT'S WHY YOU WERE LEFT HERE ON EARTH IN THE FIRST PLACE.
OF COURSE, YOU DIDN'T KNOW...
YOU WERE NOTHING BUT A DECOY!

BUT NOW THAT THE FIRST PHASE OF MY PLAN IS ALMOST COMPLETE, YOU HAVE NO FURTHER USE HERE.

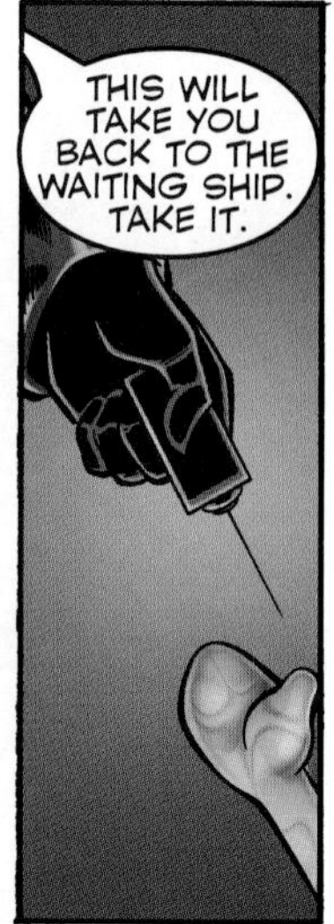
THIS WILL TAKE YOU BACK TO THE WAITING SHIP. TAKE IT.

YOU ARE A GREAT DISAPPOINTMENT AS A WARRIOR. EVEN AS A GREEN YOU SHOULD NOT HAVE FAILED THIS SIMPLE TASK.
THE REDS WILL PUNISH YOU SEVERELY. I DO NOT ENVY YOUR RETURN HOME.

AS FOR OFFICER LUCK, ONCE YOU ARE GONE, YOUR BOND WILL BE SEVERED AND HE WILL DIE.
BUT THAT DOESN'T CONCERN YOU.
NOW, GO!

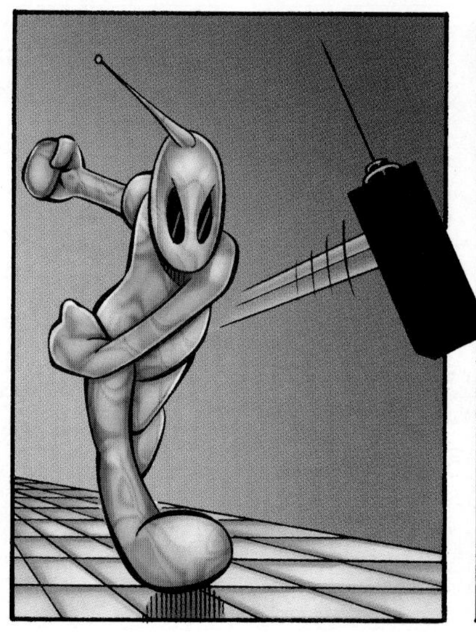

CRASH!

YOU SHOULDN'T HAVE DONE THAT LITTLE ONE. NOW YOU WILL HAVE TO DIE WITH YOUR FRIEND.

BUZZ!

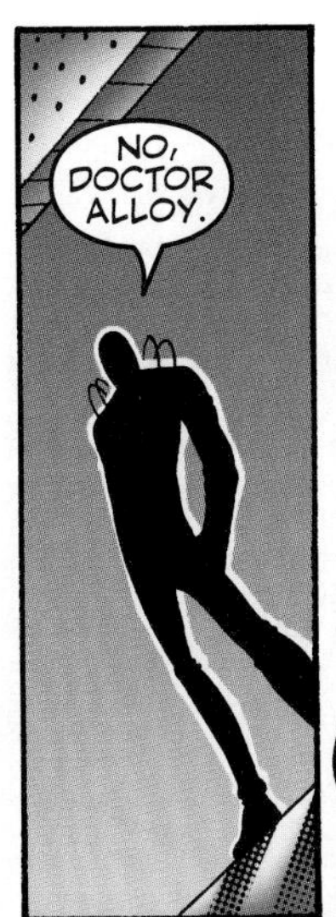
NO, DOCTOR ALLOY.

THEY WILL NOT DIE. NOT YET.

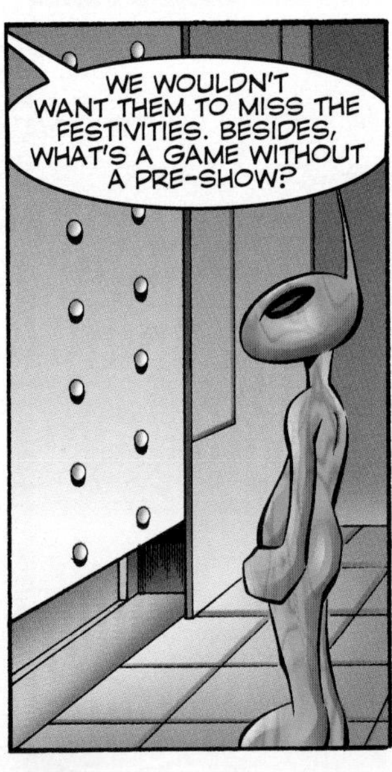
WE WOULDN'T WANT THEM TO MISS THE FESTIVITIES. BESIDES, WHAT'S A GAME WITHOUT A PRE-SHOW?

I DON'T LIKE HIM.

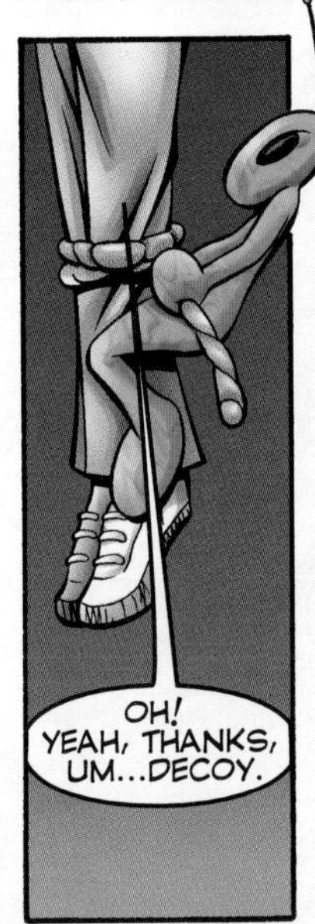
OH! YEAH, THANKS, UM...DECOY.

MIND IF I CALL YOU THAT? I DON'T THINK I'LL EVER BE ABLE TO PRONOUNCE YOUR REAL NAME.

HOW LONG WAS I UP THERE FOR? COULDN'T HAVE BEEN THAT LONG IF THE BOMBS HAVEN'T GONE OFF YET.

NOW TO GET US OUT OF HERE.

BUT HOW?

THERE'S NO DOOR AND THAT'S A LOT OF DEAD WEIGHT.

YEAH, WHAT IS IT?
Oh...
my...

RUN!
KA-CHINK
CLANK!
TAT-TA-TAT-TA-TAT-TA
CLINK!
CLINK!
CLINK!
I, UH, THINK YOU JUST MADE HIM MAD.

Um, Decoy...

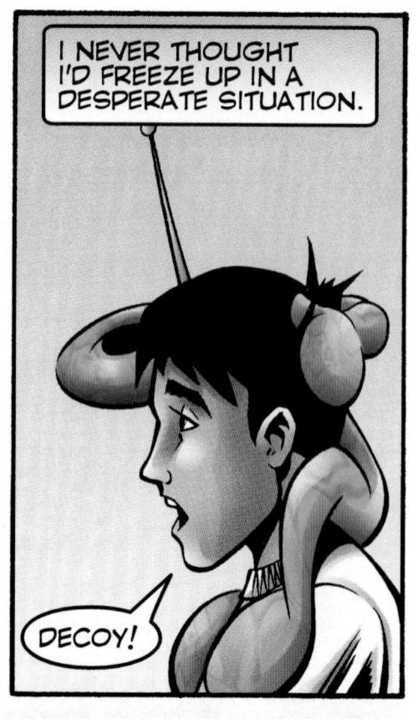
I NEVER THOUGHT I'D FREEZE UP IN A DESPERATE SITUATION.
DECOY!

DECOY!!!

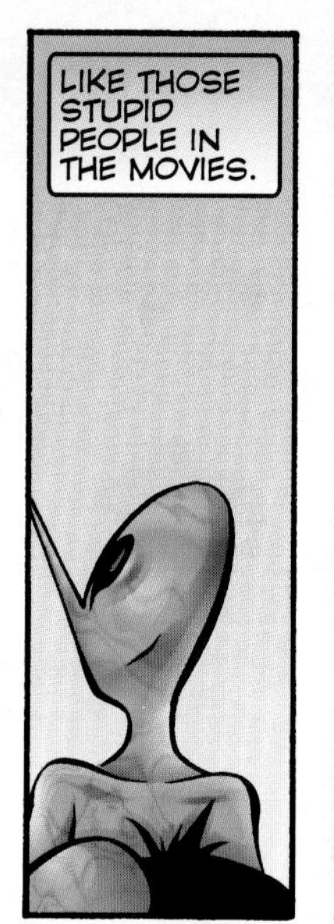
LIKE THOSE STUPID PEOPLE IN THE MOVIES.

GOES TO SHOW WHAT I KNOW.
SCHOOP

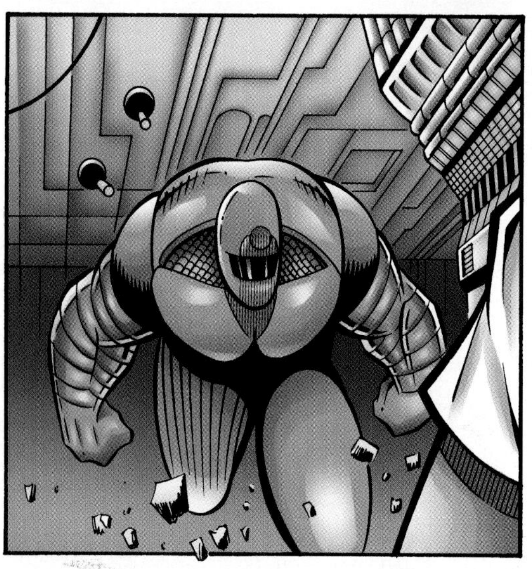

THANK GOODNESS FOR DECOY.
WHOOSH

I'M ALRIGHT NOW-- I CAN DO THIS.

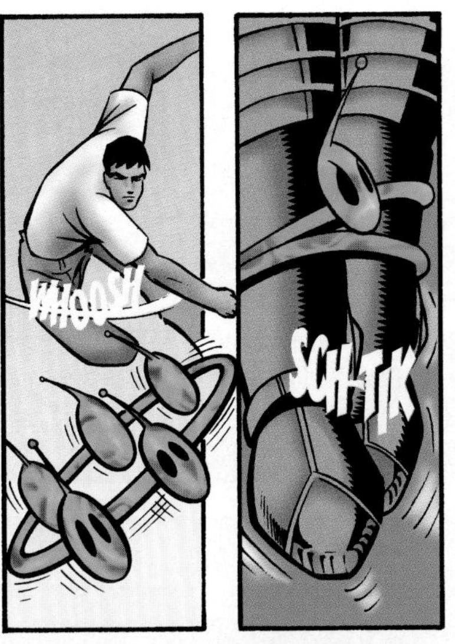
WHOOSH
SCH-TIK

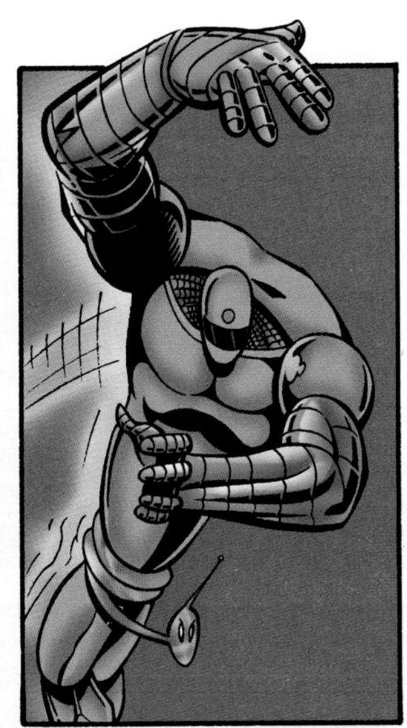

THOOM!

WELL, THERE'S OUR WAY OUT.

BUT FIRST, WE'VE GOTTA TAKE CARE OF ONE SMALL DETAIL.

MALLET, PLEASE!

ADMIRABLE SHOW OFFICER LUCK.
VERY CLEVER.

SO WHY DON'T YOU AND ALLOY COME AND CONGRATULATE ME IN PERSON?

IT'S QUITE SIMPLE, OFFICER--IF WE DID THAT, WE'D MISS THE BIG EVENT.
IT'S SET TO BEGIN SHORTLY.

YOU'RE TOO LATE.

THE WALL--HE CAN ESCAPE.
LET HIM GO. BY THE TIME HE GETS ANYWHERE THE POLICE DEPARTMENT WILL BE IN SHAMBLES AND I'LL BE TAKING OVER THE CITY.
SOON WE CAN MOVE INTO THE SECOND PHASE.

--AND HERE WE ARE, LIVE, WHERE DOLPHIN CITY IS ABOUT TO LAUNCH ITSELF INTO THE TWENTYFIRST CENTURY WITH A NEW AND HIGHLY ADVANCED COMMUNICATION SYSTEM.

NICE VIEW.

CAN SEE ALMOST EVERYTHING FROM UP HERE.

HELLO THERE, MR. WATERSON.

GIVE ME JUST ONE REASON TO WASTE YOU.

NO ONE REALLY SEEMS TO APPRECIATE THE ART OF VIOLENCE ANYMORE.

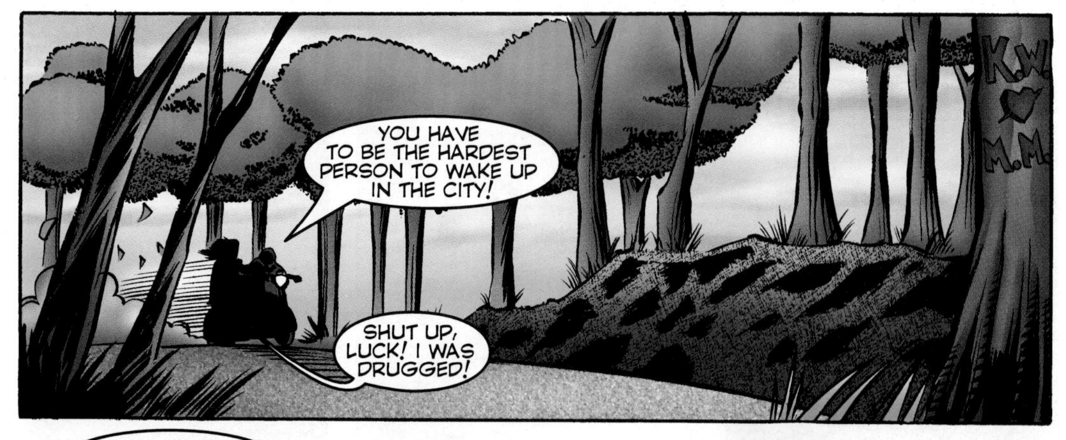

YOU HAVE TO BE THE HARDEST PERSON TO WAKE UP IN THE CITY!
SHUT UP, LUCK! I WAS DRUGGED!
K.W.
M.M.

SO WAS I AND I DIDN'T SLEEP THROUGH...
ALIENS SITED
CAN'T YOU GET THIS STUPID, LITTLE HAMSTER POWERED BIKE GOING? PRESS THAT SPEED BUTTON OF YOURS!

I CAN'T-- IT TAKES UP TOO MUCH GAS AND WE'RE RUNNING LOW.

I'VE GOTTEN US THIS FAR, THOUGH, AND I'M NOT ABOUT TO GIVE UP!

ZENDELLE
DON'T WORRY, WE'RE ALMOST THERE.
WHO IS HE!

TESTING, TESTING...HELLO? CAN YOU HEAR ME?

EENIE

MEANIE

MINIE

MOE

KEEP ON YOUR TOES, MEN. WE DON'T WANT ANY SURPRISES.

OH, GEEZ BUDDY, LET ME DO YOU A FAVOR.

WHOA, BABY!!

BUT BLONDES ARE MORE MY TASTE.

ATTENTION!!
PUT THE FOOD DOWN!

YOU NEED ME TO HELP YOU GET THAT?

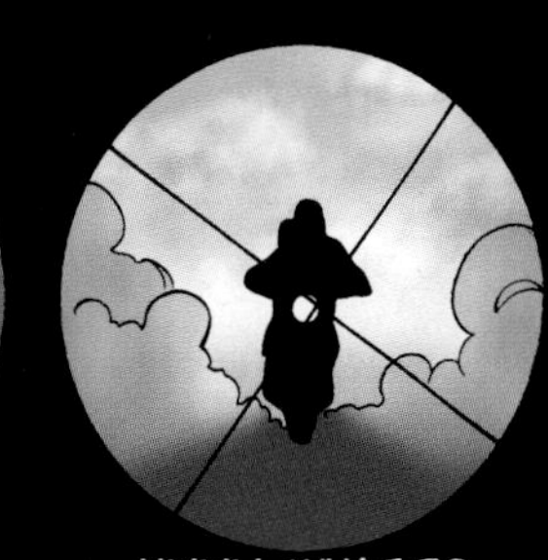
HMMM, WHAT DO WE HAVE HERE?

GOOD MORNING, LADIES AND GENTLEMEN OF DOLPHIN CITY! IN CASE YOU DON'T KNOW, I'M MAYOR PLATENBURG.
AND THIS IS THE PRESIDENT OF FUNTECH CORPORATION-- MR. WATERSON.
ARE YOU OKAY MR. WATERSON?
UHH, YES SIR. I WAS JUST GATHERING MY THOUGHTS.
WHEW! SEE, I TOLD YOU WE'D MAKE IT.
AND NOW WITHOUT FURTHER ADO--
I'M SORRY.
NOOoooooooo
CLICK

AND WATERSON HAS JUST... OH MY GOD! I CAN'T BELIEVE THIS!
2
EXPLOSIONS! ALL OVER THE CITY!
THOOM
KA-BOOM
CRASH
NO TRESPA
BOOOM
JUNK YARD

IT WAS HORRIBLE...
RUN FOR YOUR LIFE!
AHHH!
'IIEEEE!

WHERE'D WATERSON GO?
WHERE'S MY DADDY?

ASHLEY!!!

ASHLEY! YOU'RE SAFE!
DADDY!

WHAT'S GOING ON HERE?

NOW'S NOT THE TIME, MAYOR. WE HAVE IT ALL UNDER CONTROL.
BUT...

GET THE MAYOR OUT OF HERE AND HOLD WATERSON FOR QUESTIONING.
TESSA, YOU AND LUCK COME WITH ME.

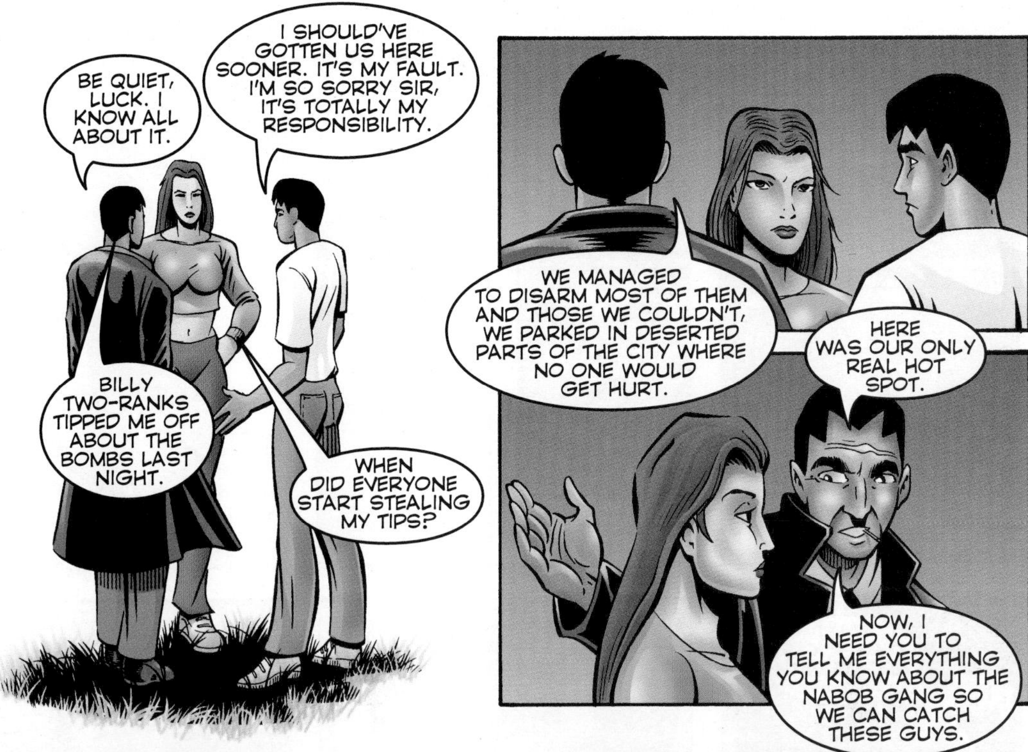
BE QUIET, LUCK. I KNOW ALL ABOUT IT.
I SHOULD'VE GOTTEN US HERE SOONER. IT'S MY FAULT. I'M SO SORRY SIR, IT'S TOTALLY MY RESPONSIBILITY.
BILLY TWO-RANKS TIPPED ME OFF ABOUT THE BOMBS LAST NIGHT.
WHEN DID EVERYONE START STEALING MY TIPS?
WE MANAGED TO DISARM MOST OF THEM AND THOSE WE COULDN'T, WE PARKED IN DESERTED PARTS OF THE CITY WHERE NO ONE WOULD GET HURT.
HERE WAS OUR ONLY REAL HOT SPOT.
NOW, I NEED YOU TO TELL ME EVERYTHING YOU KNOW ABOUT THE NABOB GANG SO WE CAN CATCH THESE GUYS.

TO TELL YOU THE TRUTH CAPTAIN, I FEEL KINDA OUT OF THE LOOP. LUCK GOT THE OTHER TIP AND YOU GOT THE LAST ONE SO...

OOOMMFF

WELL, LETS ALL GET SOMETHING TO EAT--WE HAVE A LOT OF TALKING TO DO.

NOW WHERE'D HE GO?
SEE, CAPTAIN?-- THIS IS THE KIND OF IMMATURE, UNPROFES-SIONAL ATTITUDE I'M TALKING ABOUT.

HELLO, LITTLE FLY!
I AIN'T LETTING' YA GET AWAY AGAIN!

THIS TIME I'LL TAKE IT SLOW SO YOU CAN ENJOY THE PAIN--GET IT DONE RIGHT.

GOOD IDEA.

I'LL SHOW YOU HOW IT'S DONE.

GASP!

UUUNWH!
WHAT THE HECK IS WRONG WITH YOU?

SUCKER!

EEERRGG

AAG GAAK!

EEERRRR!

WHAT THE?!

SNARL

THAT'S IT! I'M OUTTA HERE!
WANTED
WHAP!
HEY! WATCH IT!
IN THE ALLEY! IT'S IN THE ALLEY!
WELL, WHATTAYA KNOW.

I'M TELLIN' YA'!
TELL IT TO THE JUDGE.

THE MORE I GOT TO KNOW HIM, THE MORE I FELT BONDED TO HIM-- BOTH MENTALLY AND PHYSICALLY, NO PUN INTENDED.

HAHAHAHAHAHAHA

DESPITE ALL WE'D BEEN THROUGH, THAT WAS THE FIRST TIME I'D REALIZED THAT THERE WAS NO LIMIT TO WHAT WE COULD DO.

BUT I FIGURED, IT WAS ONLY A MATTER OF TIME BEFORE HE'D WANT TO *PHONE HOME*.

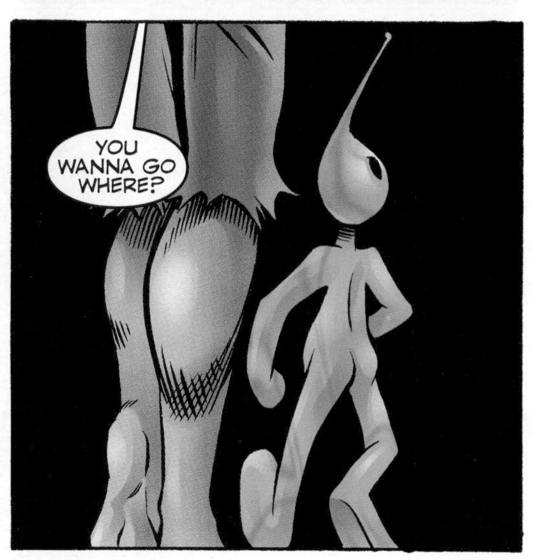
YOU WANNA GO WHERE?

DOLPHIN CITY IS LEFT STUNNED AND CONFUSED IN THE AFTERMATH OF SEVERAL EXPLOSIONS AROUND TOWN TODAY. THE CITY'S POLICE FORCE HAS YET TO OFFER AN EXPLANATION FOR THE MORE THAN 15 PATROL VEHICLES PUT OUT OF COMMISSION AS A RESULT OF THOSE EXPLOSIONS...
CAPTAIN?
GET LUCK IN HERE-- I NEED SOME ANSWERS.
PFP RULES

POLICE CAPTAIN TANNER MADE THE ENIGMATIC STATEMENT THAT WE SHOULD BE GLAD THAT THERE WERE NO MAJOR INJURIES AND THAT IT WAS ONLY 15 CARS THAT EXPLODED. HE REFUSED TO MAKE ANY FURTHER COMMENT.
FIFTEEN CARS... *IMBECILES!!!*

YOU ALRIGHT, SON? YOU LOOK A LITTLE LOST-- TALKING TO YOURSELF AND SUCH.
NOPE. THANKS, ANYWAY. I'M JUST ENJOYING THE FRESH AIR.
ECO
ALRIGHT, DECOY. THERE'S NO ONE HERE--COME ON OUT.
I CAN'T BELIEVE YOU'RE MAKING ME SIT THIS OUT.
YOU'RE NOT GONNA GO HOME...ARE YOU?
WHAT DO YOU MEAN DON'T WORRY? I COULD DIE IF YOU LEAVE!
I KNEW THERE WAS NOTHING I COULD DO TO STOP HIM IF HE REALLY WANTED TO GO. I JUST HAD TO LEAVE MY LIFE IN HIS HANDS.

MEANWHILE...
TO EMPLOY HUMANS WAS A MISTAKE.
THERE WAS AN INTERNAL LEAK SOMEWHERE.
BUT I WILL NOT FAIL NEXT TIME.
YOU *WILL* HAVE THIS PLANET IN YOUR CONTROL.
NO NEXT TIME? BUT YOU SAID BEFORE...
NO! YOU CAN'T TAKE...
NOOOOOOO

AFTER ALL WE'D BEEN THROUGH, I SHOULD'VE KNOWN HE WOULDN'T LEAVE ME.
AND SO HERE I AM...
NOW, HOW DO I EXPLAIN THIS TO CAPT. TANNER?
THE END?

GALLERY OF DECOYRATIONS*:

COVER BY MARC GABBANA

BACK COVER BY COURTNEY HUDDLESTON

* Title courtesy of F. Eugene Morton of Inglewood, CA

Art by Courtney Huddleston and Bob Almond

Art by Bruce Ingram

Art by Keith Martin and Rober Quijano

penny farthing press
By
Courtney Huddleston
SKETCH:
IDEA:
DR. A
PAGES
& QUOTES:
Yes

ERASER
CONCEPT SKETCH PAGES
SKETCH: SHRIKES
IDEA: Also a Nacrumian; The Shrikes are life long enemies to the Metas.
- Even though these guys don't look as nice & innocent as the Metas, they are actually the good guys.
- 90% of the battles between the Metas & the Shrikes have been caused by the Metas aggression & tempers.
- As mean as the Shrikes appear on the outside, they actually are very much to themselves & only fight when provoked.
- Their world would be peaceful if the Metas' thirst for dominance was nonexistant.
TAIL SPIKE - poisonous\ Causes Metas to explode
CLAWS - rips Meta skin
TEETH - strong enough to eat Metas with
COMMENTS, NOTES & QUOTES:
So far none have ever been to earth, or any other planet.
Copyright
Penny-Farth
PT SKETCH
SKETCH:
DECOY
12
T SKETCH PAGES
SKETCH:
Personality Traits
Metas
1. heartless
2. stern
3. Short tempered
4. alert
5. aggressive \ dominant
6. vengeful
Personality Traits
Decoy
1. kind
2. pleasant
3. patient
4. alert
5. leisure \ layed back
6. forgiving
Copyright 1998
Penny-Farthing Press, Inc.
perhaps the first & only
magic pencil
WEASE
Copyright 1998
Penny-Farthing Press, Inc.